"You can't study and do a job if you're pregnant. You mustn't take risks."

"Fine. I'll be careful. Jake, understand this—I am having a baby. *I am,* not *we are.*"

"You've already made that clear. But I told you before that I owe you, and I'd like to help. You have to let me support you."

"I don't have to do anything," Kelly said through gritted teeth.

"So what are you going to do for money?" Jake demanded.

"I don't know," she yelled back. "Put a lodger in my spare room. I'll think of something. But I'll tell you this, I won't be asking you for permission."

"You're brilliant! Meet your first lodger. I need somewhere to crash, and with my rent you'll be able to leave your job. It makes sense!"

Will they...?

Won't they...?

Can they...?

The possibility of parenthood: for some couples
it's a seemingly impossible dream.
For others, it's an unexpected surprise....
Or perhaps it's a planned pregnancy
that brings a husband and wife closer together...
or turns their marriage upside down?

One thing is for sure, life will never be the same
when they find themselves having a baby...maybe!

This emotionally compelling miniseries
from Harlequin Romance® will warm your heart
and bring a tear to your eye....

THE PREGNANCY BOND

Lucy Gordon

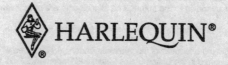

TORONTO • NEW YORK • LONDON
AMSTERDAM • PARIS • SYDNEY • HAMBURG
STOCKHOLM • ATHENS • TOKYO • MILAN • MADRID
PRAGUE • WARSAW • BUDAPEST • AUCKLAND

ISBN 0-373-03733-3

THE PREGNANCY BOND

First North American Publication 2003.

Copyright © 2002 by Lucy Gordon.

Visit us at www.eHarlequin.com

Printed in U.S.A.

CHAPTER ONE

ON KELLY'S eighth wedding anniversary she gave a party to celebrate her divorce.

Strictly speaking it was 'their' divorce, but of course Jake was missing, as he had been for most of the big events in their marriage. He probably wasn't even in the country, so it was natural that he didn't show up.

That, plus the fact that she hadn't invited him.

She had a lot to celebrate and she was going to do it in style. She'd just embarked on the college course she'd rejected eight years ago in favour of marriage, and this time she was going to stay. She was going to graduate with honours. And she was going to forget Jake Lindley had ever existed.

Not that that would be easy when his face seemed to crop up every time she turned the television on. *'Jake Lindley, reporting in the thick of the riots…. Jake Lindley digs deep and finds the truth you weren't supposed to know…'*

Jake Lindley was a hero, a handsome, hard-bodied, daredevil, sexy icon of the media age, with keen eyes and a wicked smile that said 'come hither' to every red-blooded woman within radius. But he'd broken Kelly's heart and she was well rid of him.

This was her world now, this cosy apartment filled with the friends she'd made since joining college a few weeks ago. At twenty-six she was older than most of the students, and there was also a sprinkling of the younger professors, especially the handsome Carl, her teacher on the archaeology course. He was in the middle of the floor, dancing madly, apparently with two partners at once. He waved for her to join them, and she waved back, but indicated that she had some drinks to serve first. He winked and mouthed a wolf-whistle.

'He fancies you,' said a voice at Kelly's elbow. She turned and saw Marianne, Carl's sister, sipping champagne.

'He winks at everything in skirts,' Kelly said, with perfect truth.

'You're not wearing a skirt,' Marianne said, frankly envious. 'You're wearing a skin-tight black satin trouser suit that makes me want to kill you just for being able to get into it.'

Kelly chuckled, pleased. Four months ago, when she'd thrown Jake out, she couldn't have squeezed into this revealing creation. But the misery of their break-up had destroyed her appetite, and by the time she'd pulled herself together she'd lost twenty pounds without even trying.

Her reward was a face that had developed seductive hollows beneath the cheekbones, a crystal-clear jawline, and a figure that slid into that tight black satin as though it had been crafted onto her. And she looked fantastic. She knew it. And if she hadn't known it, the yearning stares of every man there would have told her.

Marianne, a beautician by trade, had completed the transformation, cutting off the mane of hair that Kelly had kept shoulder-length ever since that long-ago day when Jake had run his fingers through it and said he liked a woman with luxurious hair. Now it was barely an inch long, nestling against her head in wispy feathers that gave her a gamine look.

In addition Marianne had ruthlessly banished the

sandy colour in favour of a glamorous red, and replaced Kelly's sedate scent with a musky perfume that was 'the new you'!

'It can't be me,' Kelly had protested, slightly shocked.

'It can be if you believe in yourself,' Marianne had insisted. 'Go for it!'

So she had, and knew almost at once that the perfume, the flaming hair and the outrageous satin suit were made for each other. Whether they were made for her she still wasn't quite sure, but it was fun finding out.

Tonight was the start of her new life as a bright single young woman, sailing once more under her maiden name, making her own way in the world instead of trailing behind a man because she loved him more than he loved her, until at last he hadn't loved her at all. As well as her looks she had rediscovered her brains, and it was like being a new person. The final pleasure was the revelation that she could be the pursued and not the pursuer.

Carl managed to pounce on her and sweep her into the dance.

'Mmm,' he murmured, inhaling her scent. 'You smell too good to be true. You look too good to be true, and you *feel—mmm*!'

'And who did you last say that to?' she asked, amused.

He was shocked. 'I lay my passion at your feet and you doubt me. Talking of your feet, I love those golden sandals.'

'Marianne made me buy them, plus the perfume. I'm really her handiwork.'

'It's not Marianne who makes you go in and out in

all the right places,' he mused, allowing his hands to move around hopefully.

'Down, Fido,' she said, wagging one gilt-taloned finger at him in mock rebuke. She liked Carl, but she hadn't quite made up her mind about him.

'All right—for the moment. You know why Marianne has got involved, don't you? She's set her heart on seeing me get married.'

'Well, she's wasting her time with me,' Kelly said with spirit. 'No more husbands, ever.'

'Was he really that bad?'

'Couldn't tell you. He no longer exists.'

'Quite right. A lover is far more exciting,' he murmured in her ear.

'Maybe, but it can't be you.'

'Why?' he demanded in comic outrage.

'You're my tutor. It wouldn't be proper.'

'I'll throw you out of the class tomorrow.'

They laughed together. He drew her close and nibbled her ear, which made her laugh even more, giving him the chance to plant a kiss on her mouth. She kissed him back. Carl was nice.

He wasn't allowed to enjoy his triumph for long. Frank, another mature student about Kelly's age, whisked her away.

'Great little place you've found here,' he yelled above the din.

'Lovely, isn't it?' she yelled back. 'Thanks for your house-warming present.' He'd given her a pair of black and white *avant garde* prints that added the finishing touch to her walls.

'How are you enjoying your freedom?' he asked.

'If I'd known it felt this good I'd have gone for it long ago.'

'Harmon is your maiden name, right?'

'Right!'

'Who was your husband?'

'It doesn't matter,' Kelly said, repeating the mantra that had sustained her through the miserable weeks. 'He's in the past.'

'Good for you. That's the only way to do it.'

When the dance ended they were by the bar. Frank danced off with somebody else while Kelly downed an orange juice.

Marianne sidled up to her. 'You really are a dark horse, aren't you?'

'How do you mean?'

'I mean that fantastic man who's just walked in; the one with come-to-bed eyes and that "I'll have any woman I like" look.'

'I don't know any man like that,' Kelly said regretfully. 'Where?'

'Over there. He looks a bit familiar. Now, where have I seen his face before?'

'On television,' Kelly said, stunned. 'And he wasn't invited.'

'Well, I'll be only too pleased to take him off your hands. Honestly, he shouldn't be allowed out alone. It's not safe—for any of us. I want everything you know. Starting with "Is he married"?'

Kelly pulled herself together. 'Not since ten-thirty this morning.'

'You mean he's—? He isn't—?'

'My ex.'

'All that was *yours*, and you let it go?'

Kelly surveyed Jake Lindley, trying to see him through Marianne's eyes. She knew about the eyes, and the look of knowing that women were clamouring for him. It wasn't his fault. Women *were* clamouring for him, and Jake had no false modesty. Or much of any kind, if the truth be told. He'd made a brilliant career as a television journalist by being accurate, hard hitting, colourful and drop-dead gorgeous.

He was thirty-two, in his prime, with a lurking devil in his eyes and a sensual quirk to his mouth that was worth any amount of good looks, except that he had them as well.

But as for him being hers? Had he ever really been hers? She'd been his in every possible way, but she'd never felt, in her heart, that she'd been vital to him. Nor had she 'let him go'. She'd merely faced the fact that in all important ways he'd gone already.

Marianne murmured, 'You really don't mind if I try my luck?'

'You're welcome to him,' Kelly said firmly. Oh, it felt good to be able to say that; not to have to watch jealously. 'Come on, I'll introduce you.'

As they weaved their way through the throng of guests Kelly tried to calm down. The sight of Jake had given her a shock because she wasn't expecting him, but that was all. She was a little annoyed with him for gate-crashing, but apart from that she was cool. A few feet away from him she waved gaily.

'Jake, how nice to see you,' she carolled.

He gave her his practised smile. 'I'm sorry, have we m—? *Kelly?*'

The sheer blank astonishment in his eyes gave her heart a lift. That had knocked him off his feet. *Yes!*

'Let me introduce you to Marianne,' she said. 'Marianne—my ex.'

'If he was mine he'd never be allowed to be an ex,' Marianne laughed, taking the hand Jake offered her.

'Kelly just discarded me,' he sighed. 'Tossed aside like an old shoe when I'd outlived my usefulness.' He was looking warmly into Marianne's eyes.

'Oh, really, Jake!' Kelly said in disgust. 'You can think of a better line than that.'

'No probs,' Marianne said hurriedly. 'That one will do just fine. Jake, why don't you come and cry on my shoulder...?'

They drifted off together. Kelly grinned unwillingly. She might have known Jake's poise couldn't be shaken for more than a moment. Whatever the place, the time, the circumstances, he could simply walk in, be instantly at home, and everyone would act as though they'd been waiting just for him. Right now, for instance, he was the only one at this party not dressed up. He wore the battered denim jeans and jacket over a black vest that he kept for travelling. Far from making him look out of place, the effect was to make everyone else seem overdressed.

His hair was shaggy and unkempt, and his skin lightly tanned. In fact he looked as if he'd just got off a plane after a long flight. Exhausting too, probably, with plenty of turbulence, which tensed him up inside, although only Kelly had ever known that. But, hey, nothing a stiff drink wouldn't put right! That was Jake for you.

Marianne had corralled him into a corner, fending off all-comers, and after only five minutes they seemed to be getting on very, very well. Kelly started to turn away, but then resolutely looked back. What he did could no longer hurt her. Besides, she had some serious flirting of her own to do, and a plentiful supply of men to help her do it.

She concentrated hard on enjoying herself, and it

was an hour before she encountered Jake again, at the drinks table.

'Just what do you think you're doing here?' she demanded.

'You said it was nice to see me.'

'I was lying.'

'Oh, great!' he complained. 'I took an early plane back to join the party, and look at the welcome I get.'

'It wasn't a welcome. You weren't invited. You ought to be shot for just marching in like this. I don't want you here.'

'Why not? It's my divorce too.' He sounded put out.

'It's a house-warming party. This is my new place.'

'Oh, yeah? You've been here three months.'

'It's taken time to do it up,' Kelly improvised. 'And it's a sort of Christmas party too—'

'Christmas is next month. But our divorce became final today.'

'Fancy you remembering.'

'I didn't,' he said in swift chagrin. 'I thought it wasn't until next week, and I—never mind! Admit it. You're celebrating getting rid of me, aren't you?'

'Yes!'

He gave her a crooked grin. 'No need to do it this way. You could have said, ''Jake—vanish!'''

'I did.'

But it was useless. He'd gone into clowning mode, which he often did when something had affected him more than he wanted to show, although she couldn't think why he was bothered about this. He'd gained the freedom from her that he'd always secretly wanted.

'You should have dropped me a hint, sweetheart,' he went on. 'I could have jumped off a bridge, vanished into the jungle—instant disappearances are my speciality.'

'You're impossible!' she said, exasperated.

'Of course I am. That's why you divorced me.'

'That and other reasons.'

'It's also why you married me.'

'Let's draw a line under that.'

'Some lines aren't so easily drawn.' For some reason there was real anger in his voice.

'You stop that,' she said swiftly. 'You messed up my life once before, but I escaped and you're not going to do it again.'

'Is that all our marriage was to you? Messing up your life? And our divorce—an escape?'

'As much for you as for me,' she said, recovering herself. 'Think how you'll enjoy your freedom now when the luscious ladies crowd around.'

'But I always came home to you,' he observed quietly.

'Eventually—yes. And I was supposed to be grateful.'

'That's not—'

He broke off, exasperated as some new arrivals interrupted them. A young woman threw her arms around Kelly and pressed a gift on her.

'This is from Harry. He's terribly sorry he couldn't get back in time, but he sends you this, and says he'll call in a few days. He misses you terribly.'

'I miss him,' Kelly said, unwrapping the gift which turned out to be a small alabaster figure, exquisite and costly. 'This is so lovely.'

More arrivals. A man said, 'Miss Harmon—'

'Kelly, please.'

'Kelly, I'm sorry to be so late—'

She said the right things and took charge of the new-comers. Jake drained his glass and the next Kelly saw he was dancing smoochily with Marianne. She gave him only the briefest glance. The days when she sat on the sideline watching Jake work the room were over.

In the early hours the party began to break up. Carl was collecting plates and glasses, taking them to the kitchen, where Frank was busily stacking the sink.

'Push off!' Carl told him. 'I've appointed myself to washing-up duty.'

'Nobody needs you,' Frank objected. 'Go home, there's a good fellow, and leave everything to me.'

'Leave Kelly alone with a predator like you?' Carl demanded.

'So who isn't a predator?' Kelly challenged, much entertained. 'You?'

At once he slipped an arm around her waist. 'I can be anything you want me to be,' he said throatily.

'Well, right now I need a kitchen maid.'

'Great. You've got me. Tell him to go. We'll do the most ecstatic washing-up the world has ever known, and afterwards—'

As he spoke he was gently pushing her backwards over his arm in a theatrical simulation of passion. He was about to drop his lips on her throat when Frank seized him by the back of the neck, howling, 'Git outta here. She's mine!'

'Don't stop him,' Kelly begged. 'I can't wait to hear about afterwards.'

But Frank grasped her by the waist, pulling her free so firmly that she staggered and had to be saved from falling by both of them.

'My afterwards is more interesting than his after-wards,' he said.

'Don't listen to him,' Carl demanded.

'You pair of maniacs,' she said, chuckling.

They stood holding her, one on each side, exchanging glares.

'I wouldn't trust either of them with your crockery,' came a voice, and Kelly looked up to see Jake lounging in the doorway, grinning. 'Clear off, both of you.'

'I can give my own orders, thank you,' Kelly said, ruffled.

'Go on, then, tell them to go.'

'When I'm ready.'

The movement of Jake's head was barely perceptible, but Carl and Frank saw it and it was enough to make them shuffle their feet and cough.

'Hey, hold on,' Kelly cried as they edged to the door. 'Ignore him. He's had no rights since ten-thirty this morning.'

'You don't need them; you've got me,' Jake said.

'Thanks, but no thanks.'

''Bye, fellers,' Jake said remorselessly.

Speechless with indignation, Kelly watched as her two admirers picked up their jackets and departed, for all the world as though Jake were the master of the house. At the door Carl turned to blow her a kiss and shrug helplessly, as if to say, What could you do?

Then she was alone with Jake.

'You've got a nerve,' she seethed. 'Ordering people out of my home. Just who do you think you are?'

'A few days ago I'd have known how to answer that, but when I arrive on our wedding anniversary and find my wife putting out the flags because the anniversary's cancelled—'

'Don't talk as though the divorce came as a surprise to you.'

'Let's say it came as a surprise that you went through with it.'

'Oh, I see. You didn't think I had the guts.'

'I didn't think you had the stupidity,' he yelled. 'Or the pig-headedness, or the short-sightedness. Where would you like me to stop?'

'Right there. You're talking nonsense. Our divorce was inevitable from the moment you slept with Olympia Statton.'

Goaded, Jake roared to heaven. 'How many times does it have to be said? *I did not sleep with Olympia.*'

'Oh, sure, you just did a little detour via her hotel room in Paris, at three in the morning, and left an hour later.'

'I've never denied I went to her hotel room—'

'Or why!'

'All right! I went in for reasons I shouldn't have done, but I changed my mind almost at once. I didn't want to turn and run like a kid who'd lost his nerve, so I hung around drinking and making excuses to talk. Then I told her I wasn't feeling well, and left. How was I to know that it was a set-up and the entire damned crew was out there timing me?'

'Luckily for me.'

'Unluckily for both of us. I didn't sleep with Olympia, but they think I did, and you listened to them, not me. Dammit, even Olympia denied it, and you as good as called her a liar to her face.'

Which was what she wanted, Kelly thought. Oh, yes, Olympia had denied it all right, but she'd done it in a way that was half an admission, shaking her head earnestly so that her blonde hair swung around her delicate features, as if to say, *You don't really think a man could resist this, do you?*

And Kelly hadn't thought anything of the kind, any more than she'd thought Jake could be alone in a bedroom with that seductive, half-clad body, and not take matters to an inevitable conclusion.

'Olympia said what you wanted,' she told Jake now. 'And later you admitted it, have you forgotten?'

'I never admitted sleeping with Olympia,' Jake said swiftly. 'In the divorce papers I admitted "adultery with an unknown woman"—'

'So that Olympia's fair name shouldn't be sullied. You're a real knight in shining armour, Jake, you know that?'

'I didn't do it for her, I did it for you—'

'From the goodness of your heart,' she said sarcastically.

'You were determined to have that divorce, one way or another. It wasn't Olympia. She was just your excuse to be rid of *me*. So I made it easy for you. If it hadn't been her it would have been something else.'

'Something or someone?'

'Whatever you've decided in that stubborn head of yours.'

'Skip it, Jake, that's all in the past. We've left it behind.'

'Oh, sure! You settled what you wanted to believe and moved on.'

'*Wanted* to believe?' She whirled on him, eyes flashing. 'If you think I wanted to believe that a man I used to love went out tom-catting then you've got rocks in your head. I believed it when I had to. And that was after years of refusing to face facts.'

'Facts? What damned facts?' he roared. 'Are you suggesting that I made a career of infidelity?'

'I've always wondered. What I did know for sure

was that I spent my time waiting for you while you took off around the world at the behest of Olympia, who always seemed to have some vital job for you when we had an anniversary or a birthday coming up.'

'Olympia is my producer; she trusted me with the assignments that made my name. I almost owe her my career—no, dammit!' He checked himself, muttering curses under his breath. 'No! What am I saying? It's you I owe things to, that time you supported me so that I had nothing to do but hunt for assignments—I haven't forgotten.'

'Yes, you have,' she said, but without rancour. She'd calmed down now. 'And why shouldn't you? It's a long time ago. Never live in the past.'

'Kelly—'

'I'm the past; she's the present—'

'Kelly, please—'

'And all our divorce did was recognise that. Now, I'm going to put the rest of the things in the sink.'

CHAPTER TWO

FOR the next few minutes Jake helped her clear away, and Kelly gave up the attempt to make him go. She washed and he dried, until at last he said, 'I don't know where to put things away in this place.'

'Leave them and sit down while I make some coffee.'

When she took the coffee in a few minutes later she found him sprawled on her sofa, dead to the world. It was a familiar sight. How often in the past had she yearned for him to return, only for him to collapse with jet-lag as soon as he walked in the door?

The clink of the cups roused him and he pulled himself upright, rubbing his eyes, then closing them again at once.

'Long flight?' she asked sympathetically.

'Ten hours. I'm dead.'

He got to his feet, yawning and stretching, and began to wander around her apartment. 'Nice,' he observed. 'Shops nearby, that little park outside, not too far from the college, just the right size.' He was opening doors as he spoke.

'Hey,' she said indignantly. 'This is my home.'

'It's all right, I'm only snooping,' he said, so innocently that it was a moment before she realised he'd admitted the offence. He'd always done that. It was how he got away with murder.

'Anyway, I already know what your bedroom looks like because people were leaving their coats here,' he

19

observed, standing in the doorway and regarding the double bed.

'Come away from there,' she said firmly.

'What's this one?' he asked, swinging around to another door. 'Let me discover your dark secrets.'

'This' was the tiny second bedroom that was filled with boxes.

'I haven't been here long and there are things I haven't found a place for,' Kelly explained. 'So tonight I just tossed them all in there. I'll get around to it soon.'

'That's not like you,' he observed, letting her lead him away.

'What isn't?'

'Leaving things. You were always so tidy.'

'I guess my priorities have changed. I'm too busy to fuss about things these days.'

Jake sat down and immediately moved to reach for something that had been sticking into his back. It was a book.

'Hey, what's this?' he demanded, studying it. *'Moving On, In Bed and In Life!'*

'Marianne gave it to me,' she chuckled. 'It's one of those New Age psychobabble things. Just a laugh.'

'A laugh, eh? And all these bookmarks? Are those the places where you're laughing hardest? Or did Marianne put them there?'

'Some are hers, some mine.'

'Which is which?'

'Work it out. You met her tonight. The way you two danced you must know her very well by now. You should have followed up. She's ready to move on and, goodness knows, *you* must be. Did she give you her number? Because if not I can—'

'Will you let me organise my own sex-life?' he demanded, harassed. 'And what does this mean?' He was stabbing the book which was open at a chapter headed 'Time For a Toy Boy?' 'Did she mark this?'

'No, Marianne's done toy boys,' Kelly said cheerfully. 'If she wanted another one she wouldn't be bothering with you. Let's face it, Jake. You hardly qualify, do you? What are you? Thirty-eight?'

'Thirty-two, as you well know.'

'Are you sure? I've always thought—I mean you look—well, anyway, thirty-two is still past your best, and—'

'All right, all right,' he said, grimly appreciative of this wit at his expense. 'So I take it the bookmark's yours?'

She glanced over and shrugged. 'Sure.'

'Nice reading matter you go in for, Mrs Lindley,' he said scathingly.

'Miss Harmon, and it's none of your business what I read.'

He recited aloud. '"Don't be half-hearted about the change you're making. Feel the sense of liberation as you chuck out unwanted possessions"—would that include unwanted husbands, by any chance?'

'Oh, don't be a dog in the manger. You were bored to tears with me. You're just mad because I made the first move to end our marriage—unless, of course, you consider Olympia the first move, which you *could*—'

'Do not,' he said dangerously, 'mention her again.'

Kelly shrugged. 'OK. Nuff said—about everything. Give me back my book.'

'Wait, I haven't finished. Where was I? "Unwanted possessions. Replace them with something as different as possible. A change of partners works wonders. If years of sex with the same man has left you feeling bored—'' now we're coming to it ''—your new lover should be somebody young. He'll bring freshness and novelty to your bed, as well as strength, vigour, and a sense of adventure.''' He set the book down. 'You must be older than I realised. I wouldn't have thought you'd reached the age for a toy boy.'

'Shows how wrong you can be,' she teased, running her hands over the tight black satin. 'Underneath this I'm all droop and sag.'

'Let me check the facts.'

'You've seen the facts plenty of times,' she said, fending off his hopeful hand.

'Not *these* facts, I haven't.'

'Well, look your fill of the outside, because that's all you'll ever see again.'

His eyes glinted. 'Wanna bet?'

'Jake! Do I look as though I was born yesterday?'

'That's what I'm trying to find out.'

'I'm warning you. Keep your distance.'

'All right. Let's get back to the subject. Toy boy.'

'I don't have a toy boy—yet. I was just planning for the future.'

'And this?' He'd found a new source of outrage in the book. '''If you're tired of the old self, try a new one—or several new ones.'' Oh, that's great. How the devil are you supposed to know which ''you'' is on duty today?'

'Easy. You give them each their own name.'

'So I see. You've written a list of names in the margin. Yvonne—'

'Sporty,' Kelly said at once. 'Likes the wind in her hair.'

'Helena—'

'Soulful and dreamy.' Kelly was enjoying herself. 'An intense inner life and a hectic imagination.'

'Carlotta?'

'A party animal. Always ready for a new experience.'

'Don't the fellers get confused?'

'Not if you keep one personality for each man.'

He stirred his coffee, not looking at her. Suddenly he growled, 'So which of them are you sleeping with?'

'*What?*'

'Carl, or Frank? Or the mysterious Harry who "misses you terribly"?'

'Get lost!'

'Or is it one of the other guys who were undressing you with his eyes tonight? Not that that would take much doing.'

'Now you're being offensive.'

'No way. I like a woman who's wise to herself. If you've got it, flaunt it. You've got it—and, boy, do you know how to flaunt it! That's OK. You missed out a whole stage of life by marrying me, I know. I don't begrudge you your fun.'

'It wouldn't make any difference if you did,' she said pointedly.

'Not since ten-thirty this morning.'

'Further back than that. In fact, not since— Oh, don't let's go down that path again. We'd end up quarrelling and what's the point?'

'So you're not going to answer my question?'

'What question?'

'Who are you sleeping with?'

She turned slightly, resting her arm on the back of the sofa, and smiled. 'Mind your own business, Jake.'

He acknowledged this with a quirk of the mouth. 'I'm still in the habit of thinking you *are* my business.'

'You'll get used to things being different,' she told him, charming and implacable.

He allowed one finger to trail across the bare skin of her shoulder. 'I'll say things are different,' he murmured, his eyes on her breasts, their shape emphasised by the shine of the black satin. 'I could get jealous.'

The admiration in his eyes was frank, and for a moment the old Kelly, the one who jumped for joy at his slightest attention, lived again. But the new Kelly firmly sat on her. She knew every trick in Jake's book, and once you could see the strings being pulled you were safe. Right?

With a face full of amusement she said, 'Don't waste your time, Jake.'

'Sure I'm wasting my time?'

'Quite sure.'

'So it *is* one of them?'

'You're wasting your time again.'

He removed his hand. 'I guess things really are different. You used to tell me everything.'

'That was when I never had anything interesting to tell. I'd hunt around in my mind trying to find something about the house or my job that wouldn't bore you rigid when you'd just come back from Egypt or Burundi, or wherever. Then you'd go on TV and talk about fascinating things in faraway places, and I'd think, Heavens, I told him about my argument with the dustman!'

'Maybe I liked hearing about the dustman. It was real. It kept me down to earth.'

'And maybe I got tired of just being your "down to

earth''. You did all the flying for both of us. I was just earth-bound.'

'I didn't even know you tonight,' he complained. 'I left a librarian and I came back to the last of the red hot mommas.'

'Not mommas,' she said quickly. 'Not red hot or any other kind.'

He frowned. Then her meaning hit him.

'I'm sorry,' he said with a sigh. 'It slipped out without my thinking. I didn't realise it still hurt you so much after all this time.'

'Yes, it's seven years ago. I should have forgotten all about it,' she said tensely. 'Like you.'

'That's not fair. I haven't forgotten that we nearly had a child. A child I wanted very much, by the way.'

'Yes, enough to marry me just because I was pregnant,' she said quietly. She didn't add what she was thinking, *And that was the only reason.*

Perhaps wisely, he decided not to answer this. 'Anyway, I meant the "red hot" bit,' he said. 'You really set the room alight this evening. Maybe I should stand in line behind Carl and Frank, and half a dozen others.'

'No, you were at the head of the queue, but your time has been and gone. It's over.'

'But how "over" can it be when people have meant that much to each other for eight years?'

'Now you're being sentimental,' she said firmly. 'You meant "that much" to me, but I meant very little to you.'

'That's not true.'

'Yes, it is. Jake, this is probably the last time we'll ever meet, so just for once let's be totally honest. Let's get the facts straight before we draw a line under them and move out of each other's lives. You married me because I was pregnant and you believed in "doing the decent thing".'

'There was a bit more to it than that—'

'Yes,' she conceded, 'you really wanted a baby. You couldn't wait to be a father. It was one of the nicest things about you. And if I'd had the baby maybe we'd have been happy. But I didn't. I miscarried in the fourth month, and I've never managed to get pregnant since.'

'Not for lack of trying,' he mused.

'We tried and tried, but I guess that was my one shot and it'll never happen again. And you still want to be a father, don't you?'

'It would be nice,' he agreed after a silence. 'But maybe it's not meant to be.'

'It *isn't* meant to be—for us. But your next wife will probably give you a dozen.'

'Don't talk about my "next wife" like that. We haven't been divorced twenty-four hours and already you're marrying me off.'

'I'm saying that we've both moved on, and that's good.'

'And what have you moved on to?'

'Archaeology. I'm an academic now.'

'And no doubt you'll be spending your vacations on digs—with Carl. Good plan. It'll keep the others wondering.'

Kelly merely raised her eyebrows. Jake frowned, trying to decipher that look. It threw him off balance not to be able to read her easily. Just who was this woman?

'Enjoying yourself, are you?' he demanded.

'You've already agreed that I'm entitled to.'

'Just be careful, that's all. I've got my doubts about some of the men here tonight.'

'I've got my doubts about just one,' she riposted.

'Hey, you really snap back at a guy these days,' he said, nettled. 'Except when you won't answer him at all, that is. Faxes, e-mails, letters—you name it. I sent it, you ignored it.'

'I didn't ignore them all. I answered at first, but I stopped when it was clear you weren't listening to what I said.'

'That was because you made me mad by not letting me pay you anything. You gave up college to help out with my career. You're entitled to a big chunk of what I make, and I'll bet your lawyer told you the same.'

'Oh, he's as mad at me as you are,' she confirmed.

'I told him, "Anything she wants". And you made him write back saying you didn't want anything from me. Boy, that was a great moment! And I'll tell you an even better one—when I found out that you'd taken a job. A real dead-end job after all the other dead-end jobs you took to help me! How can you get a good degree if you're wearing yourself out working as well? You supported me in the lean years. You should at least let me support you through college.'

'Why should I?'

'Because I owe you that,' he said angrily. 'And I like to pay my debts.'

Kelly regarded him levelly. 'If you think of our marriage as a debt to be paid off, then we're further apart than I thought. You'll never understand, will you?'

He wanted to slam something against the wall, preferably his own head. No, he didn't understand, and he was furious with her and himself. He wasn't trying to 'pay her off', only to express his gratitude and appreciation for all she'd done for him. And it had come out all wrong, as so often with him. Before a news camera he was at ease, the words pouring out in a golden flow. But with this one person he was tongue-tied and clumsy.

'Then explain it to me,' he said through gritted teeth.

'What I did, I did because I loved you. We were a team. Remember how we told ourselves that?'

'Of course I remember. But it didn't work out much of a deal for you, did it?'

'I wasn't making deals,' she said quietly. 'I was doing something for the man I loved. What I forgot—or was too young to know—was that two people who think they're doing the same thing never really are. Not quite.'

'I don't understand,' he said flatly. 'I never could follow when you talked like that. I'm a plain man and I see things plainly. I don't think that was ever enough for you.'

'I only meant that you saw our marriage differently from me.'

'I did you an injustice,' he said, clinging to the one thing that was clear to him. 'And I'm trying to put it right.'

'But you can't put the past right. You can't make it something it wasn't. It's dead and gone.'

His combative streak would have made him fight that view, but there was something melancholy about 'dead and gone' that silenced him. He'd never been able to cope with her subtler wits. Handling facts was easier for him, and somehow it had always been tempting to use them to evade an argument. After a while Kelly had given up trying to make him talk things through, and he'd been relieved.

Kelly gave a little sigh. 'Oh, well,' she said. 'No point in arguing now.'

'Perhaps I want to argue,' he said illogically.

Her lips twitched. 'Nonsense, Jake, you never wanted to argue. You just wanted me to keep quiet and agree with you. Failing agreement, keep quiet anyway.'

'You make me sound like a monster,' he said, appalled. 'A bully.'

'No,' she said with a touch of wistfulness. 'You weren't either. Just a man who always thought he was right. Much like all the others, really. No worse, anyway.'

This faint praise did nothing to appease him.

'Have you been thinking like this all the time?' he demanded.

'Not all of it, no. But it wasn't much of a marriage at the end, was it?' She began gathering cups and headed for the kitchen. 'No, stay there.' She stopped him rising. 'There isn't much.'

She wanted to get away from him. The conversation had taken a turn that she was finding hard to cope with. She should never have started talking about love with Jake. It aroused memories best forgotten.

But do I really want to forget? she asked herself wistfully. *Would I wipe out the last eight years? I know they took a great deal away from me, but they gave me so much.*

She remembered herself at seventeen, a schoolgirl, slightly overweight, shy, lonely, earnest, not laughing enough. She'd worked hard at school, driven by dreams of escape from the dreary little provincial town and the single mother who'd resented her. Mildred Harmon had still been in her thirties, 'with my own life to live', a phrase she'd used often and with meaning.

The last year at school had been punctuated by various lectures about career options. Kelly's sights were set on a brilliant college career, but she'd attended the meeting about journalism, expecting to see Harry Buckworth, editor of the local rag, whom she knew slightly. But Harry had gone down with flu. Instead he'd sent Jake, who'd been on the paper a year.

And that was it. All over in a moment. The twenty-four-year-old Jake had been like a young god to the ultra-serious schoolgirl. Tall, lean, jeans-clad, spinning words like the devil. And such words: a fine yet powerful web of bright colours that turned the schoolroom into a magic cave. And he'd laughed. How he'd laughed! And how wonderfully rich and free it had sounded. She could have loved him for that alone.

Afterwards she'd strolled home in a dream, scheming how to meet him again, so oblivious to her surroundings that she'd collided with someone, and been halfway through her apology before she'd realised it was him.

He'd taken her for a milk shake and listened while she talked. She didn't know what she'd said, but when they'd left the evening light had been fading and she'd returned home nervously, wondering how she would explain her absence. But the house had been empty and cold. On the kitchen table there had been a note from her mother, out with her latest boyfriend, telling her to microwave something for herself.

After that they'd seemed to bump into each other a lot, just by chance. The meetings had followed a pattern. Milk shake, talk, stroll home. Sometimes he'd helped with her school projects, looking up facts, guiding her to useful web sites, letting her bounce her ideas off him. Or he would discuss his assignments in a way that had made her feel very grown up.

Once they'd reached her home to find Mildred peer-

ing through the curtains and beckoning them in. She'd
looked Jake up and down thoughtfully, and when he'd
left, said to her daughter,

'Watch out for him. You're becoming a pretty girl.'

She didn't know how to say that Jake had never so
much as kissed her, but two weeks later, on her eigh-
teenth birthday he finally did so, taking her into seventh
heaven.

'I was waiting for you to be old enough,' he said.

Life was brilliant then. Mildred, evidently feeling
she'd done her motherly duty, was out more than she
was in, and Kelly was free to indulge her happiness.

Then Jake had lost his job.

'I had to fire him,' Harry explained when Kelly but-
tonholed him. 'He's a hard worker, I admit, but by
golly he's an opinionated young devil.'

'A good journalist needs opinions,' Kelly protested,
parroting Jake. 'And he shouldn't be afraid to stand by
them.'

'Standing by them is one thing. Riding roughshod
over everyone is another. There was this assignment,
an important one—I told him how it should be handled,
and he just went his own way, wouldn't take advice. I
had to be away for a day and when I came back the
paper was nearly to bed. If it had gone in like that it
would have offended our biggest advertiser—'

'Advertisers!' Kelly said scornfully.

'That's him talking,' Harry said. 'He's brash,
thoughtless, and he's got more mouth than sense.'

And it was true, Kelly thought now, standing in her
kitchen eight years later. *Brash, opinionated, cocky, in-
sufferable. When he got in front of a camera it all
turned to gold, but we couldn't have known that then.
And I knew him when he wasn't like that...*

She forced herself back to reality. She'd promised herself not to hark back to the past, and it was time to be firm and drive Jake out. She returned to the living room, ready to deliver the speech that would send him away. But it died on her lips.

Jake was where she'd left him on the sofa. The jet-lag had caught up with him again and he looked as if he'd passed out the moment she left him. That was how he'd always been, she reflected. He spun his web of words, he slept, he passed on. And she should have remembered that.

It was good that he'd slipped away from her yet again. It got things in perspective.

CHAPTER THREE

SHE fetched a blanket from the cupboard and gently draped it over him. Then she turned out the lights and made her way to her bedroom, but no sooner had she closed the door when a loud thump made her open it again. In the half-light from her bedroom she could see Jake on the floor.

'Hell!' he said, shaking his head. 'What was that?'

'You turned over too far and fell off the sofa,' she said.

'Uh-huh!' He yawned and rubbed his eyes.

She rearranged the cushions and when he'd hoisted himself back up she began to take off his shoes. 'Let's get you comfortable,' she said, swinging his legs back into position and drawing the blanket up.

'Are you going to tuck me up?' he asked with a grin.

In the near darkness she could discern little about his face except the mischievous gleam in his eyes. The likeness to a cheeky kid was so clear that she assumed a motherly, teasing tone. 'Yes, I am, so you be good.'

'I'm always good.'

'Yeah. Sure. 'Night.'

She wasn't sure how he did it, but one moment his arms were safely tucked under the blanket and the next they were around her waist.

'Don't I get a goodnight kiss?'

'No,' she said, although he was already pulling her near. 'Jake, this isn't just goodnight. It's goodbye.'

'A goodbye kiss, then.'

One last time couldn't do any harm, she promised herself as he drew her closer. She was armoured against him now, and this was a good way to prove it.

The shape of his mouth was a shock. She knew it well, yet somehow it felt unfamiliar. It seemed such a long time since she'd last felt it against her own. There had been no kissing in the last weeks of their marriage. She'd seen his mouth tight with exasperation, and finally hard with anger. Now it was firmly purposeful, yet gentle, as she'd first loved it. She'd longed for that gentleness and had thought she would never know it again. Suddenly it was returned to her, like a present, and she couldn't give it up just yet. She would enjoy it for a moment, and be strong later.

They kissed like strangers exploring new territory, intrigued, ready to be surprised, even more ready to follow the dancing light of desire. His mouth was eager against hers, even a little predatory in a way that thrilled her. Lips that were purposefully seductive, arms like steel bands, hands that were tender even as they imprisoned her: this was Jake at his most overwhelming.

Into her mind crept the unwanted memory of Craig—Craig somebody—who'd had the temerity to whisk a scoop from under Jake's nose. He'd smiled pleasantly, stood Craig a drink, acted the good loser. But the following week he'd trumped him with a much bigger scoop that turned Craig's story into small potatoes.

'I'm not a good loser,' he'd explained.

Kelly had divorced him, rejected him in the eyes of the world, made him look like a loser. No way was he going to leave without reclaiming her. Even if nobody else suspected, the two of them would know, and that would be enough for him.

So the moment to be strong was now. Not later, now. And she would manage it—in just a moment. Something in the movements of his lips was making her resolution slip away. His tongue teased her, flickering against her mouth, urging her not to be a spoilsport. It began to seem ridiculous not to do something she really wanted so much, and suddenly her mouth was open to him, inviting him to explore, for his own delight and hers.

The tip of his tongue, wickedly caressing her inner cheek, sent delicious tremors through her. Too late for caution now, she thought, challenging him back. Wherever this led, she had no choice but to follow. She moved in slowly, taking control of the kiss, surprising him. She could feel his astonishment in her flesh, in her bones.

After a few minutes of intense mutual enjoyment he drew away, regarding her. His eyebrows were raised, giving him a quizzical look.

'Hmm,' he said, considering. 'Yvonne? Helena?'

She drew a swift breath. 'Carlotta,' she said, greatly daring.

'Well, that's what I thought—hoped—because she sounds such an interesting lady.'

'You don't know just how interesting,' she murmured with a little chuckle. 'Not that she lets everyone in on the secret.'

'Always ready for a new experience,' he repeated her words from earlier in the evening.

'Ready for anything,' she confirmed.

Jake took her at her word, letting his hands drift very slowly over her body, thinly covered in tight black

satin. A few brief touches were enough to confirm his
suspicions that she wore nothing underneath, but there
was no way he was stopping at brief touches. A woman
dressed like this for only one reason: to tempt a man
to undress her. That was fine, as long as he was the
man.

Kelly was holding her breath as he explored her
shape. They had made love so often before but, by the
way he was causing her to feel, this could have been
the first time. She knew he was relishing her as almost
a different woman, which made him different in his
turn.

When he touched her top, seeking for a way to open
it, she helped him by finding the little silver button that
connected with the zip. Slowly he drew it down, revealing the soft swell of her breasts, then tossed the
top away, releasing them completely to his entranced
gaze.

For a moment he laid his face between her breasts,
while she clasped her hands behind his head. The first
flicker of his tongue against her skin was so subtle that
she barely felt it. But it came again and again, growing
more intent with each movement so that she arched her
back, inviting him, offering herself to him with movements that he couldn't possibly mistake.

When she felt the tip of his tongue curl about one
peaked nipple she let out a long, long sigh of bliss and
threw her arms high over her head.

'What do you want?' he murmured against her skin.

'You know what I want.'

'Tell me.'

'I want—everything.' She could hardly speak the
words for the excitement streaming through her.

He rose upright, his hands on her waist, so that she
was lifted high above him. He lowered her a little so

that her breasts touched his face again, and carried her like that to her bed, kneeling on it and cradling her as she slipped down onto the sheet. Urgent fingers moved against her skin and she felt the trouser suit sliding down past her waist, her hips, down until he could toss it away and reveal her nakedness.

His own clothes followed fast, leaving her in no doubt of one thing. His control was vanishing fast. He wanted her beyond thought or reason, and it was no surprise when he slipped quickly between her thighs and claimed her vigorously. It had been so long since they'd lain together that it was only when Kelly felt him inside her that she knew how badly she wanted him. For a few blinding minutes she blissfully gave as good as she got, satisfying a body that had been starved of passion and letting out a long sigh of fulfilment when her moment came.

The sensation was so intense that she closed her eyes for several minutes while her head swam. Her heart was beating violently and she lay still for several minutes as her whole body calmed down. It was like sleeping and yet not sleeping. She was somewhere else, watching herself as if from a distance, wondering if this could be dull little Kelly who'd lost her husband because she bored him.

When she opened her eyes she found Jake had left her and was standing, naked, by the window. For a brief moment she felt abandoned, then something about the tension of his body made her realise that this was different. His head rested against the window frame, and she had just enough of a sideways view to see that his eyes were focused on a far distance deep inside himself.

That in itself was curious. Jake had never been a man for introspection. He'd always said that the outside world kept him fully occupied. Analysing, wondering about himself—these weren't his style. It had been an article of faith with the young Kelly that her adored Jake wasn't afraid of anything. Otherwise she might have thought he was afraid to know who he was.

But she couldn't think of that. Now she was the one who pushed thoughts aside to enjoy the purely physical. She was still suffused with delight from the best sex she'd ever enjoyed, and its glow transformed the world. She leaned back against the pillows, revelling in the sight of Jake's long, straight back, narrow hips and taut buttocks. There was so much power in those hips, she thought with a little remembering smile: power to drive into her again and again, sending the pleasure mounting to unimaginable heights.

She let her eyes drift over him, lingering on his thighs, lean but muscular, tense with whipcord strength. The brash, eager boy she'd loved had grown into somebody else, just as the Kelly of old had gone for ever. In her place was a woman capable of regarding a man from one simple, basic angle, and sizing him up critically.

And he passed the most critical test, she had to admit, smiling even more broadly.

So far.

For she had more tests in store for him. This was no longer lovemaking, if it had ever been. This was something she'd thought never to experience with Jake—sex for the sake of it. Simple erotic enjoyment with no purpose except sensual delight, and the enjoyment of new experience.

She slipped quietly out of bed and padded across the room until she was just behind him. When she rested her fingers lightly on his back he raised his head, but didn't turn it. Kelly's touch drifted softly down the length of his back until it reached the base of his spine, paused for a moment, then continued purposefully. She let her fingers wander where they would, advancing and retreating, feeling his mounting desire, playing with it.

He half turned but she prevented him. 'No,' she whispered against the warm skin of his back. 'I'll let you know when.'

Her fingers had reached the front and were engaged on skilful work. She could feel that he was ready for her again. Vigorous as his exertions had been, she could bring him back to life, and the knowledge thrilled her.

'I thought you were still asleep,' he murmured.

'Do you still think so?' she said, pressing herself against him so that he could feel the hard peaks of her nipples against his back.

'I don't know what to think. Perhaps you're a phantom.'

'Could a phantom do this?' she asked, making frisky movements across his chest with her fingers. 'And this?' she added, enjoying his groan and the way he pressed back against her so that her hands slid down again, found their target, homed in. *'Or this?'*

'What the devil are you doing?' he demanded huskily.

'Proving that I'm no phantom. On the contrary, I'm very, very physical.'

'You sure as hell are,' he gasped, relishing the devastating skill that had taken him by surprise. 'No woman—that I know—could do *that!*'

'That's right—no woman that you know,' she agreed. Here was the best part of this delightful game. The selves they were tonight had no past and no future. They had come out of nowhere and tomorrow would dissolve into nothing. But tonight they existed, and felt, and burned with desire. It was heady magic.

She wondered how long he would stand there, letting her work on him, and she soon had her answer. With a groan that showed her that she'd got the better of him, he twisted swiftly around and claimed the initiative.

'Ready for anything?' he muttered against her lips.

'I think I could give you a surprise or two.'

But just now he was surprising her, and she was loving it. In their marriage Jake had always been a tender, considerate lover. But now there was nothing tender in his grasp, and not much that was considerate as he pulled her down onto the bed in a way that brooked no argument. He parted her legs and was inside her swiftly, sending fierce waves of piercing heat and light through her. After the first shock she wrapped her legs about him and drove back, as hot and wild as he, and as demanding. She had been made for this, and it was only now that she knew.

After the first fierce drive he made his movements slower, and so did she, so that they teased each other with delay. Kelly was astonished at her own control. It seemed to come from an unexplored region in her, perhaps the same place where grief had lived and endured until finally endurance was too much.

She'd thought she knew her own nature—sedate, modest, long-suffering, but not sparky or adventurous. Now she was astonished to discover a tiny imp of resentment, almost revenge, as though her searing sexuality was telling him, *So there!*

If so it was reprehensible, but there was no doubt it was giving him something to think about.

When they'd fought each other to a standstill, and

he was breathing heavily, he reached swiftly over and switched on the bedside lamp.

'I want to look at you,' he said.

At once she rose and knelt on the bed, stretching her arms high so that her small, firm breasts were shown for his delectation. Those lost pounds were a godsend, she thought, as she swayed this way and that, displaying herself to him, as shameless as a wood nymph.

'Is that what you wanted to see?' she asked wickedly.

'It's more than my best hope. Woman, do you know that you're not safe?'

She laughed. 'It's too late now to be worrying about that!'

'That is sheer provocation,' he declared, clasping his hands about her waist, where they almost met.

There was a glint in his eye that was intriguing her more every moment. Glancing down his length, she saw that she'd done him an injustice. Resisting his attempts to toss her onto her back, she moved over him.

'There's more than one new experience,' she teased, easing herself into position and enjoying the shock on his face. 'Relax, enjoy.'

'I'd like to know where you learned to do this,' he growled, gasping a little between words.

She leaned down and whispered softly in his ear. 'That's none of your business.'

It was incredible what you could learn from books these days, but she wasn't going to tell him that. How good it was to feel him inside her in a different way, newly thrilling, an unexpected kind of excitement. And, most wonderful of all, to gaze down on his face, and see by its thunderstruck look that, for once, the 'little woman' hadn't done just as he would have predicted.

At last it was over and she flung herself down beside him, feeling as though she could laugh with the gods.

One thought pervaded her. He might think he'd reclaimed her, but in truth she had reclaimed him, and with him, her freedom.

Now she could let him go.

The room was brilliant with the light of morning, and she sat up sharply, awake, cold, clear-headed and exasperated with herself. The sight of Jake's sleeping form beside her made her groan.

What had she done? She might have guessed he'd try a trick like this. He was piqued that she'd divorced him, so he'd set out to prove he could carry her back to bed anyway. Now she was a scalp on his belt.

It didn't matter that she'd just enjoyed the best sex with him that she'd ever known. It had been blinding, ecstatic, wonderful. Of course it had. Last night he'd seen her as a new woman, in demand among men, and the predator in him had jumped to the head of the queue.

She slipped out of bed, put on a robe and went into the kitchen, seemingly occupied, but actually straining her ears for the sound of him, and at last she heard him pad barefoot across her front room. She looked around, smiling brightly.

'Breakfast coming up,' she sang out. 'Have this to be going on with.' She pressed a mug of coffee into his hand.

'How are you?' he asked, watching her carefully.

'Wonderful, considering that party. I thought I might have a hangover, but I'm fine.'

'I don't think you drank very much.'

'Just a little bit tipsy,' she said untruthfully.

'Then you've changed. You never used to drink much.'

'I never used to go in for one-night stands either, but for you I made an exception, for old times' sake.'

'That was nice of you,' he said quietly.

'Well, you owed me some fun after sending Carl and Frank away before I made up my mind about them.'

Jake took a swift breath. 'Don't talk like that.'

'Hey, lighten up,' she chided. 'It was great. And it was the perfect way to end our marriage. No hard feelings and a good time was had by all.' A horrid thought seemed to strike her. 'Jake, you *did* have a good time, didn't you?'

'I had an incredible time,' he said quietly. 'I hadn't realised you'd grown so—skilled.'

He seemed to be trying to read her face, but Kelly blocked his enquiring eyes with a bland smile that concealed how hard her heart was beating.

'You're right, Kelly,' he said at last. 'You're a new woman. I hadn't quite understood that. I suppose I still saw you in the old way, but not any more. Your life's your own now. You took it back, and you're going to make it whatever you want.'

'Best for both of us,' she said.

'Yeah! Best for both of us. It's just that I—'

She held herself tense for what he would say next. Almost as though it mattered. He seemed to be struggling with the words, but soon he would say them, and she would know...

Then his face changed as he saw something over her shoulder, and everything vanished from his expression but horror. '*Oh, ye gods!*' he yelled, his eyes on the clock. 'The time! Look at the time.'

'It's just past ten. Why?'

'I need a cab ten minutes ago. Who can I call?'

'I'll do it.'

'I have to catch the midday flight or my name will be mud.'

She would never know now what he might have said. The next few minutes were taken up with calling the cab, while he dressed frantically. He finished just as her doorbell rang.

''Bye,' he said, kissing her cheek on the run. 'There's a present for you on the bed. Combined Christmas and house-warming.'

The gift was a watch, made of platinum and studded with tiny diamonds. It was the sort of thing a man might buy in the duty free shop at an airport when he was running out of time. Kelly was an expert in that sort of gift because Jake had always bought her one when he returned home from the other side of the world, and she'd never told him how lonely she was when he was away, because it would have been churlish to complain to a man who'd bought her a costly gift. Besides, she'd been almost as lonely when he was there.

But this was different. There was no need for him to have bought her anything, and the gesture touched her. Smiling, she looked around at the room where he'd so lately been.

Then her smile faded as she saw how empty it was, a bleak emptiness that seeped into her heart until it felt like a stone crushing her.

CHAPTER FOUR

KELLY had approached college prepared to discover that her brain was rusty, and she'd been fooling herself for years. Instead she found the course fascinating and easy to follow. The tutors praised her work and she was popular with them and her fellow students. In many ways this was the ideal college life of her dreams.

The only fly in the ointment was the need to work to make ends meet. She'd taken a bank loan to cover most of the fees, and worked three evenings a week in a small café. It was proving more tiring than she'd thought. At the end of the day she longed to return to her little home instead of spending the evening inhaling greasy odours and being rushed off her feet.

Perhaps she should have taken up Jake's offer of financial help so that she could leave the job and never again have to smell cooking oil, which was making her nauseous these days. Working at the café hadn't been so terrible before, but meeting Jake again seemed to have left her in a strange mood. Her normally equable temper had been replaced by an irritability that could flare into annoyance without warning.

She'd heard no more from him after he'd rushed away that morning, and she was glad of that because it made it easier to draw a line under the business. Once more for old times' sake, and no sentimentality on either side.

But it wasn't that easy. What had happened between

them in her bed had felt less like a goodbye than a hello. That was how people enjoyed each other at the start of something, seeking out and conquering new territory, putting down markers for the future. It was absurd to make love like that at the end.

Absurd. Cling to the thought. Laughable. Ridiculous. Idiotic. Words like that would help deaden what threatened to be an ache in her breast.

She knew that Jake had returned from wherever he'd dashed off to because she'd opened a newspaper to see a photograph of him, leaving a glamorous media party. Olympia was on his arm, smiling and looking impossibly gorgeous. Apart from that, if she wanted to see him she watched the television news, which was pretty much what she'd been doing for the last few years.

One evening she was just catching up with the headlines before going to bed, and there he was, looking out of the screen, while a voice-over intoned, 'Jake Lindley talks to us, live, from war-torn—'

Kelly yawned sleepily, not hearing the rest. Wherever Jake was reporting from, it was fairly sure to be 'war-torn'. He'd always been happiest in the thick of the action, and she'd sat at home terrified for him, and keeping her worries to herself when he returned. It bored him to talk about dangers he regarded as non-existent.

'It's all hype, darling,' he'd often said. 'I never actually get hurt, do I?'

And it was true, he didn't. It was pleasant not to have to worry because he was nothing to do with her any more.

She had to admit that he looked good on camera, his bronzed skin suggesting a man of action, and his shaggy hair slightly lifted by the breeze as he made his report in a brisk voice.

'Tonight the two sides seem as far apart as ever—accusations—fierce denials—nobody quite knows—'

She barely heard. All her attention was fixed on Jake's face. When had that little frownline appeared between his eyes? She tried to remember if it had been there last time, but his face as it had been then refused to come into focus. There were too many impressions pulling in different directions.

'The sound of gunfire never ceases—there behind me, and all around—'

Jake's voice stopped suddenly and Kelly came out of her reverie to realise that he'd vanished from the screen. The camera was swinging around wildly, somebody was shouting, and there was Jake on the ground, with people running towards him and an ugly red stain seeping between his fingers, which were clutched to his stomach. Only then did she realise that he'd been shot.

He was still talking to camera, and incredibly managed a painful smile. 'I guess they were closer than I realised—' He went on talking, grimacing with pain as people lifted him and raced away from the gunfire, refusing to stop doing his job, until he fainted.

The broadcast returned to the studio. Nobody seemed to know exactly what had happened. Kelly could have screamed.

She snatched up the phone, then dropped it again. She was no longer Jake's wife, and had no more right to information than anyone else. But she could feel her whole body going cold with shock as she stared at the set, willing it to tell her something.

She tried the text pages, but the broadcast had been

live and it was too soon for anything to be posted. She changed channels, hoping one of the others had picked it up. For an hour she sat there, flicking from place to place, feeling as though she was going mad.

When she couldn't stand it any longer she dialled the studio and asked for Dave Hadway, who worked in the newsroom and whom she knew slightly. But Dave had left the company, and instead Kelly found herself talking to Olympia Statton.

'This is Kelly,' she said, forcing herself to speak calmly. 'Is there any news of Jake?'

'He's been taken to the local hospital out there,' Olympia said.

'How bad is it?'

'I'm sorry, we're not releasing that information to the public.'

Kelly lost her temper. 'What do you mean, ''the public''?' she raged. 'I used to be married to him, as you very well know.'

'I do indeed, but you went your separate ways,' came Olympia's self-satisfied voice. 'I'm sorry, Miss Harmon, I'm afraid I can only discuss Jake's condition with his family.'

'But he has no family,' Kelly cried.

'He has people who care for him.' The line clicked dead.

Kelly replaced the receiver forcefully. Then she did something she'd never done before in the whole of her well-regulated life. She picked up a vase and hurled it at the far wall with all the force she could manage. It disintegrated into a hundred pieces. Cleaning them up gave her something to do.

She sat up into the small hours, gathering crumbs of information from the television. The shooting was shown again and again. She watched it obsessively. There was Jake, standing so assured before the camera, and she wanted to seize him and keep him safe. But she never could, and he always fell to the ground, still gamely talking.

As the night wore on she learned that although the terrain was remote the local hospital was efficient and had managed to stabilise Jake, but his condition was still critical. Still in front of the set, she fell asleep from exhaustion, and awoke to find the morning half over.

The central heating had gone off and she was stiff and cold, with an aching head that swam as she forced herself out of the chair. She sat down again at once, and stayed there until the world had settled back into place. When it was safe to move she rose and put on the heating, then staggered into the kitchen to make herself some hot tea. She needed food inside her after that upsetting night, she decided. But after cooking eggs and bacon she threw it away, untasted. She couldn't face grease. In fact she couldn't face anything until she knew that Jake was safe.

She sank back into the chair, castigating herself for her weak will. What had happened to independence and putting him behind her? All gone for nothing, because he was hurt.

And something else bothered her. Olympia had called her 'Miss Harmon'. She not only knew that Kelly had resumed her maiden name, but she also knew what it was. And only one person could have told her. Kelly reckoned that said it all.

The next day a flying ambulance conveyed Jake out of the country where he'd been wounded and to the nearest large hospital, in southern Italy, for an operation to remove the bullet. After that there was silence, and Kelly was forced to assume that no news was good news.

Now her life was lived permanently on the rack. She tried some mutual friends, but they knew little more than she did herself. The only information came from Olympia, who gave an interview to a tabloid newspaper called, *Jake Lindley, the man I know*. The resulting piece put Olympia firmly in the spotlight, while hinting at the depth of her relationship with Jake, who, she was quick to state, had recently divorced. The only thing missing was an announcement of their coming wedding. Kelly wondered if they would dispense with that, since they were clearly lovers already.

Finally Kelly struck lucky with a fellow journalist, who told her Jake had called him and asked for some books to be brought to the London hospital where he would arrive at the end of the week. He was out of danger now, and was being sent home to complete his recovery.

Kelly knew the hospital, which was only a few miles from where she lived. It was unnerving to have Jake so close and yet know nothing about him. She tried telephoning but found that all calls were being diverted to the television company's press office.

Well, it was none of her business anyway. They'd said goodbye, and that was it. Kelly told herself that very firmly, and was still telling herself as she set out, one afternoon, for the hospital.

As she entered its doors she was expecting a rough passage, but her luck was in. The young woman on the desk beamed at the sight of her.

'Don't tell me, let me guess,' she said. 'Jake Lindley. You're his wife. I saw you on the telly last year. You were sitting next to him when he collected that award for "TV newsman of the year". It is you, isn't it? I mean, your hair's different, but—'

'Yes, it's me,' Kelly said. 'But we're divorced now.'

'I know. I read it in the paper. I don't like that other one. She swans in here like Lady Muck, laying down the law.' She became conspiratorial. 'Third floor. Room 303.'

'Thank you,' Kelly said fervently, and sped off before anyone could stop her.

On the third floor she almost lost her nerve. Olympia would be there, comforting and beautiful at the bedside. Jake's ex-wife would be an unwelcome intruder. Then she set her jaw. If her presence embarrassed Jake she would leave, but she wasn't going without seeing him. She reached Room 303, took a deep breath, and quietly opened the door.

At first glance the room was a riot of cheerfulness. There were cards everywhere, some with funny pictures, some depicting flowers. There were real flowers too, of all kinds, with a large bouquet of red roses claiming centre stage. No prize for guessing who'd sent those, Kelly thought.

But after the first moment her impression of gaiety died, partly because the room was eerily quiet. A man lay on the pillows, staring blankly ahead. There were no books on the bed, or anywhere near him. No radio or television broke the silence, and he seemed engulfed in a weariness so profound that it had blotted out the world. No way was this Jake, who was never happy unless active.

Then he turned his head, and Kelly drew in her breath. It was Jake, yet not Jake. Suddenly she remembered the last time she'd seen his face on a pillow, gazing up at her naked body, his eyes alight with appreciation, devilment and shock. Now he had the dreary greyish pallor of someone who'd come too close to death. His cheeks were sunk, his eyes lifeless, and he looked as if he was on the edge of despair.

How could a man change so much in a short time? she thought wildly. *Let him get well! She would give anything if only he could be himself again.*

She waited for the smile of recognition, but the sight of her produced no gleam, and for a dreadful moment she was afraid his mind had been affected. But then he said very quietly, 'Is it you?'

She hurried forward to the side of the bed, leaning over him. 'Yes, it's me. Jake, do you know me?'

At that he gave a faint smile. 'Don't worry. It was my stomach they caught, not my head. I'm no crazier now than I always was. It's good to see you, Kelly. I was sure you'd come.'

The simple statement shocked her. She should have been here long ago.

She pulled up a chair and sat beside the bed, taking his hand in hers, horrified at how thin it felt.

'I'd have been here sooner but you're a hard man to reach these days. I only got this far because the receptionist downstairs saw us together on TV. Will Olympia walk in on us, trailing photographers?'

He gave a slight grin. 'You read that piece? Hilarious, wasn't it? I don't blame her for grabbing a little publicity. She's on her way to the top.'

And Jake admired people who did that, she remembered. 'High-octane lives', he'd called them, summing up a world of glamour, excitement and above all, achievement. Kelly knew that she could never be called high-octane. She doubted that she was even two-star.

'She won't be here today,' Jake went on. 'She's away on a management course.'

Obviously producing wasn't going to be good enough for Olympia Statton. She was aiming for executive status, head of a news-gathering empire, with Jake Lindley as her anchor man.

'I expect you're dying to get back to work,' she said.

'Why do you say that?'

'You were always the world's worst patient, getting out of bed long before you should.'

'They encourage me to get out of bed for a while each day. The problem is walking. They got me one of those supports old people use. I said "No way, I can walk by myself." But when I tried I wobbled and had to be saved by a nurse who was half my size. And Dr Ainsley, who's a great surgeon but has the bedside manner of a piranha said, "I told you so. Now stop acting the giddy fool!" So I did.'

'You don't mean you've found someone who can talk some sense into you?' she said with a tender smile.

'Didn't have any choice. My legs were giving way under me. It cured me of rushing things.'

The despondency in his voice made her ask sympathetically, 'Feeling out of it?'

'A bit. Olympia calls me on the phone, just to keep me in touch with what's going on—'

'Jake, you don't have to explain to me,' she said hurriedly. 'Your private life is your own.'

'Yeah, sure,' he said after a moment, and withdrew his hand from hers, leaving her with the sad sensation of having snubbed a man who couldn't take it. And again the thought ran through her head. This is Jake?

'You're not short of well-wishers,' she said, indicating the cards.

'No, the guys at the studio send me rude cards almost every day. Trouble is, some of them are really funny and I'm not allowed to laugh. And I get cards from the public. I try to write back but—' He shrugged.

She noticed the pile of unopened mail by his bed. One letter lay half in and half out of the envelope, as though he'd starting opening it and lost interest.

He made a sudden resolute movement, pushing back the bedclothes. 'Let's get out of here. I'll buy you some tea and cakes in the café.'

'Are you supposed to do that?'

'Sure. Gentle exercise—whatever that means—is good for me. I've been up already today, but I got tired and went back to bed.'

Her unease increased. How often had they argued because he'd refused to admit he was ill? She would have enjoyed nursing him, but her attempts had irked him! 'Molly-coddling', he'd called it. Now he sat, wryly acquiescent, as she helped him on with his dressing gown, and actually asked her to fit his slippers on his feet, as leaning down was difficult for him.

She looked around for his walker, but could see only a wheelchair. 'This?'

'Stuff that!' he said, showing a flash of the old Jake. 'I can walk now.'

He slipped his arm through hers and they set off. How thin he was! He'd never carried any spare flesh, but now she could feel the bones of his arm against her. Not just thin, she thought with horror. Frail.

He talked cheerfully about Dr Ainsley, making him sound all kinds of a dragon. But despite his brave air she could feel him flagging. The café was some distance away, and he was obviously glad when they reached it and he could sit down while she went to the self-service counter.

'What are you allowed to eat?' she asked.

'Not much. For a long time I was fed through tubes. Now I'm allowed baby food, mostly liquid. You could get me a banana milk shake now, and maybe a strawberry one later.'

'Just banana and strawberry milk shake?' she echoed, aghast, remembering his cavalier way with a whisky and soda.

'No, I'm allowed chocolate milk shake as well, and even ice cream if I'm feeling adventurous. Life is full of variety around here.' He grinned, looking more like his normal self.

When Kelly returned from the counter Jake was flirting with a pretty waitress. The sight cheered her up.

She had a milk shake too, to keep him company, and as they sat sipping through straws he said wryly, 'We look like a couple of high-school kids.'

'If you go back a while. High-school kids don't drink milk shakes any more.'

'True. But we did, once. You were seventeen, but you looked younger, so it had to be a milk bar.'

'Oh, yes,' she breathed as it came back to her. 'I'd taken an exam and you were waiting outside the school gates.' She chuckled suddenly.

'What?'

'You asked how the exam had gone. You were only being polite, but I was on such a high that I bent your ear for half an hour about how brilliantly I'd done. Then I looked at you suddenly and you were glassy-eyed with boredom.'

'Not boredom. I admit I was barely listening, but I was thinking how pretty you were.'

'And I thought how grown-up you were, until you made a gurgling noise with your straw,' she remembered.

'Like this?'

He'd reached the end of the glass and he noisily sucked up the last bubbles through the straw. She immediately did the same, and he grinned. Then something caught his attention over her shoulder. Kelly turned to see a tall man standing in the door, scanning the room until he saw Jake. The next moment he was making his way towards them.

'I looked into your room and you weren't there,' he said. 'I hoped I'd find you here.'

'Kelly, this is Dr Ainsley,' Jake said, and she reached up to shake hands.

She was trying to equate this pleasant-faced man in his forties with the dragon of Jake's description. Dr Ainsley had a stubborn chin but genial eyes.

'I've heard all about you,' he said cheerfully, engulfing her hand. 'Anna, on Reception, spread it through the building as soon as you'd left the front desk.'

'Ah,' she said, non-committally, wishing she knew exactly what Anna had said.

'Let me get you a coffee,' Jake offered.

'I'll get it,' Kelly said at once, but Dr Ainsley laid his hand on her arm.

'Let him,' he said. 'It'll do him good to move about.'

When Jake was out of earshot the doctor said quickly, 'I wanted to talk to you alone.'

'How is he, really?'

'He's recovering, but not as fast as he should. It's as though he can't rouse himself to make the effort.'

'But he's always been so strong and confident, so—so macho.'

'They can be the worst. The more a man is used to being in control, the harder it hits him when he's in a situation he *can't* control. Psychologically he's in deep shock at discovering that he can't just make this go away by will-power.'

'He told me how he tried to walk alone too soon.'

'That was the turning point. Until then he'd managed to convince himself that he could get well to his own timetable. When he discovered that he was wrong it hit him very hard. He's going to need careful looking after.'

The significant way he was regarding her made Kelly say hastily, 'Dr Ainsley, I'm not married to Jake any more.'

His face fell. 'But I thought—I must have got it wrong.'

'We were divorced a few weeks ago. If we were still married, do you think I'd have waited this long to come?'

'Of course not. I'm sorry.'

'Jake's in my past.'

'But you're here.'

'Caring for him is a habit that's hard to break. Just not in that way.'

'I gather he doesn't have any other family.'

Kelly shook her head. 'No brothers or sisters, and his parents are dead. And since neither of them had siblings either, he's got nobody.'

'Except you.'

'And Olympia Statton.'

'Ah yes! Glamorous blonde, all furs, teeth and la-di-dah?'

Kelly choked with delight at this put-down of Olympia. 'That's her.'

'She's been in once or twice, carefully timed for when the cameras were there. Then she complains about "press intrusion". She's not exactly chaining herself to his bed. Anyway, what Jake needs now isn't a lover, it's a mother or a sister.'

'All right, I'll come in as often as I can.'

Jake had returned with the coffee. He looked drawn, as though the short trip had been too much for him.

'You shouldn't have done it after walking here,' Kelly said, concerned.

'I'm all right,' he said irritably, then quickly, 'Sorry, sorry. Didn't mean to snap.'

It was almost as though he needed to placate her, she thought, shocked. During their marriage he'd often apologised for some piece of thoughtlessness, but never as though he was actually afraid to offend her. But before she could reassure him he made a sound of annoyance with himself.

'I forgot the spoon.'

'I'll get it,' Kelly said, rising and putting a restraining hand on his shoulder.

'I'm perfectly capable—'

'No, you're not, so shut up!' she told him firmly.

He didn't argue further, and there was a touch of gratitude in his grin.

She fetched the spoon and returned to the table, but just as she was sitting down everything seemed to retreat from her. She reached out quickly and just managed to sit down before she fell.

'What is it?' Jake asked anxiously.

'Nothing, I—' Kelly covered her eyes because the room was swimming.

'Don't say nothing. I thought you were going to faint.'

'Well, I'm not,' she said, pulling herself together. 'I'm just a bit tired these days.'

'Well, if you will insist on working in a café as well as going to college—'

'Yes, I expect it's that,' she said, trying to sound cheerful through the waves of nausea.

Jake studied her face, concerned. 'I don't like it. You're a funny colour, isn't she, doc?'

'Not really,' Dr Ainsley said with a shrug. 'It's the strip lighting. It makes everyone look pretty ghastly.'

Which was remarkably unperceptive of him, Kelly thought, because she felt terrible.

'I'll be back in a moment,' she said hurriedly, and made a dash for it.

There was a ladies' room nearby, but by the time she reached it the nausea was already passing. She found a chair and leaned miserably back against the wall, until she felt well enough to move. When she went out the two men were waiting for her.

'Are you all right?' Jake asked.

'She's fine,' Dr Ainsley said. 'Look, her colour's better already. It's you I'm worried about. Let's get you back to bed.'

He commandeered a wheelchair and came back to the ward with them. There he said briefly to Kelly, 'Not more than five minutes,' and departed.

'Give that job up,' Jake said, as he climbed carefully into bed. 'I know what you said before, but we're not enemies, are we?'

'Would I be here today if we were?'

'Then let me help you, even if it's just a loan—'

'I'll come in tomorrow and we'll talk about it then,' she said. Just now she felt she had to get away to think.

'Tomorrow, then,' he agreed. He suddenly tightened his hand on hers. 'You will come, won't you?'

'Promise.'

After a moment's hesitation she kissed his cheek and hurried away.

In the corridor outside, Dr Ainsley was waiting for her.

'I think we should talk,' he said.

CHAPTER FIVE

'YOU'RE wrong,' Kelly said with a touch of defiance. 'I'm not pregnant.'

They were sitting in Dr Ainsley's consulting room. He'd steered her straight there, brooking no refusal, and pressed a cup of hot, strong tea on her. When she was feeling better he'd dropped his bombshell.

'Just because I had a little giddy spell...' she said, almost annoyed with him.

'I admit I'm not certain,' he agreed. 'But I'm a doctor. You develop an instinct. My instinct says you're pregnant.'

'But I can't be.'

'Do you mean that literally? There hasn't been anyone—?' He paused delicately. 'It would be understandable if you'd celebrated your new freedom—'

'I did that, all right,' she groaned. 'I celebrated my new freedom with my old husband. But you don't understand. I was pregnant before, years ago, and miscarried. Ever since then I've tried hard to start another child, but no luck. I simply don't believe that it happened the one time I wasn't thinking about it.'

'But that's *why* it happened. Doctors see it all the time with couples who've been childless for years, then they adopt and within six months the wife conceives. Having the adopted baby to love makes her relax, and when she stops being tense about it—' he spread his hands in an expressive gesture '—it happens.'

'But you're only guessing,' Kelly said with more firmness than she felt.

He took something from a cupboard. 'Here's a testing kit. Why don't we talk again in a few minutes? There's a bathroom through there.'

She clung to her belief in a mistake until the last moment, and then it felt as though she'd always really known.

'I guess I should have trusted your instinct,' she agreed, emerging and showing him the test strip. 'Oh, this can't be happening! Jake and I are finished.'

'You don't think he'd be pleased?'

'He mustn't know. He's moved on. So have I.'

'Have you?' Dr Ainsley asked with raised eyebrows.

'Yes. Even if I manage not to miscarry—oh, it's complicated. Promise me you won't tell him.'

'Of course, but don't forget he saw what happened just now. He may get suspicious.'

'I don't think so. Jake's terribly good with facts but he doesn't notice much about people.'

At home that evening she tried to concentrate on archaeology, but soon gave up. How could she think about ancient constructions when the entire construction of her own life was being turned upside down?

A baby, when she'd abandoned all hope long ago! Jake's baby, when it was too late for it to save their marriage! Bitter, bitter irony!

She'd told Dr Ainsley that she couldn't be pregnant, and suddenly she could see herself at eighteen, saying exactly the same thing to an exasperated Mildred.

'Of course you could,' her mother had replied. 'That's what *I* said, and I was wrong. I was only sixteen when it happened to me. You held out until eighteen. Well done, girl. You're a credit to the family.'

'Mum!' she'd protested.

'You've got to face facts. I suppose it's Jake's?'

'Of course it's Jake's. I love him.'

'Let's hope you have more luck with him than I had with your father. Once he knew you were on the way I never saw him again.'

But Jake had been different. To Kelly's incredulous delight he'd been overjoyed about the baby.

'How fast can we get married?' had been his first question.

'Wait—wait—' she said, half-crying, half-laughing with joy.

'Of course we can't wait. Let's set the date now.'

'But you haven't asked me to marry you,' she pointed out.

'I'll ask you later. Let's get going.'

And before she knew it she was a bride, dressed in a neat blue dress that would be useful later. They married so quickly that her waist hadn't even started to thicken.

Mildred was laconic and practical.

'You're a fool, girl. You got top marks in those exam results, and you could have done anything. Well, you've blown it and that's that. I'd saved a bit of money to help you through college, but you'll need it now.'

The cheque was generous, but Kelly didn't read too much into it. Mildred was clearing her conscience, and it was no surprise when, a week after the wedding, she took off with a lorry driver and passed out of her daughter's life.

She was too happy with Jake to care. Their first married home was two rented rooms, in which he wrote freelance pieces and she struggled against sickness. She became grumpy, but Jake could always laugh her out of her 'down' moods, and nothing could spoil her joy. She was carrying Jake's child, totally in love, and passionately grateful to him for wanting her and their baby, even if she did suspect that it was the baby that was the main attraction.

He told her of his lonely childhood without brothers or sisters.

'We moved around a lot with Dad's job, so I never got the chance to make friends. I kept wanting my parents to have more children so that I'd have someone to play with. But they never did. Then when I was fourteen they died.'

'So now you think you're going to get someone to play with?' she teased.

And he grinned and said, 'Reckon that's it.'

Now she was carrying his child again, as unplanned and unexpected as before. But nothing else was the same.

She wondered how she could have missed the clues. But years of failing to conceive again had convinced her that it wasn't possible, so the signs had slid past unnoticed, or at least misinterpreted. The tetchy mood that she recalled from last time had returned, but she'd mistaken it for the strain of working so hard.

Here she was at the beginning of her 'new life', and suddenly she was back in the old one.

'No,' she muttered aloud. 'I've played this script before and I'm not doing it again. I get pregnant, Jake does the decent thing, and I'm left feeling grateful. Not this time. No way. I'm a big girl now. I'll look after myself and my baby without help from him.'

My baby! It had a melancholy sound. It should have been 'our baby'. There were so many moments that she was going to miss: telling Jake that he would be a father at last, seeing his eyes glow with joy, sharing the birth with him.

She must forget about all those things, because Jake didn't really want her. He'd wanted the glamorous creature of the party, but that hadn't been the real Kelly. Even the pencil-slim figure would soon blur and thicken.

But for how long? Suppose she miscarried again? That, too, she would face alone if it happened. And it was better that way.

'He needn't even know I'm pregnant,' she went on to herself. 'I'll say I have to work, and not visit him again. He'll go back to Olympia and I—' She pressed her hand over her stomach, the fingers splayed, and a smile came over her face.

Suddenly it hit her. She was going to have a baby, Jake's baby, the child she'd waited, longed and prayed for, all these years. Her smile was not only one of tenderness. It was a smile of triumph.

This was the true beginning of her new life, not as the sexy imp who'd briefly captured Jake's volatile fancy, but as a strong woman who could cope alone, depending on no man.

'Who says it's too late?' she whispered. 'It might be too late for us, but it's only just starting for me.'

Next day she found Jake sitting in a chair by the window. He seemed stronger, but there was a tension about him that made conversation difficult.

'Does the doctor think you're any better?' she asked.

'I'm making progress. Slow but sure, that's what he keeps saying.'

'Good.'

'What about you?'

'I'm fine. I got a good mark for my last essay.'

'And your job?'

'That's easy.'

'But for how much longer?' he asked slowly.

Time seemed to stop. 'What—do you mean?' Kelly asked.

'You're pregnant, aren't you?'

'What? Jake, for pity's sake—one little giddy spell—'

'At precisely three o'clock in the afternoon.'

'I don't understand.'

'That's what happened last time. Dead on three o'clock.'

She stared. 'You can't possibly remember that.'

'We were hurrying to catch a bus. It left at ten past three and when we reached the bus station I said, "It's only three o'clock." And the next minute you turned green. Yesterday it was three o'clock again.'

'Well—that's a coincidence.'

'You're pregnant.'

This was the last thing she'd expected. How had Jake remembered that detail all these years when she hadn't remembered it herself? With disaster staring her in the face she tried belligerence. 'Well, what if I am?'

'I just thought you might want to tell me,' Jake said, looking out of the window.

'Why?'

He digested the implications of this for a moment before saying quietly, 'No reason.'

'Let's stick to what we agreed, Jake,' she said desperately. 'Friendly, but no strings.'

'All right, then as one friend to another tell me what happens now. Are you planning to marry the father?'

'That doesn't concern you.'

'Tell me,' he insisted, like the old, determined Jake.

'No.'

'Live with him?'

'No.'

'Your decision or his?'

'Mine.'

'Who is he?'

'Jake, I'm warning you—'

'Do you even know who he is?'

'What did you say?'

'Well, let's face it, you were spoilt for choice when I last saw you—*Kelly*!'

He was talking to empty air. Kelly had stormed out.

She ran most of the way home, driven by her anger. She stopped finally in a tiny park where there was a duckpond, and sat on a bench. How shrewdly she'd planned a way of dealing with the situation, and then she'd fallen at the first fence.

Yet she'd still travelled far. Once she would have been in tears at this point. Now she didn't want to cry. She wanted to wring Jake's neck. How dared he suspect her of sleeping around? Even if she had worked hard to give him that impression.

A mother duck, with six frantically paddling ducklings in tow, made her way determinedly across the pond. Kelly smiled at the sight, and felt herself calming down. As her thoughts regained some sort of order she realised that Jake might have done her a favour by doubting the baby's parentage.

He'd seen her 'belle of the ball' act, and been fooled by it. Good. Anything was better than having him suspect that he was still the only man she'd ever slept with. What he was thinking would make life simpler. The truth would merely make it impossible.

Her courage was returning as she headed out of the park.

When she reached her apartment the telephone was already ringing.

'I'm sorry,' Jake said as soon as she answered. 'I really didn't mean it the way it came out. It was just that you— Never mind. Can you come back here?'

'No, but I'll look in tomorrow.'

'Promise?' His voice was urgent.

'I promise.'

He was answering letters when she arrived next day, but he shoved the whole lot aside to greet her eagerly. His colour was better and his voice stronger.

'How are you feeling?' he demanded.

'Fine.'

'Have you seen your local doctor?'

'No.'

'Why, for Pete's sake?' His eyes narrowed with sudden suspicion. 'Have you made any decisions yet?'

'Yes,' she said, understanding him. 'I'm going to have the baby. I want it.'

He relaxed slightly. 'Then you must take proper care of yourself. You'll just have to take money from me after all.'

At the words 'have to' Kelly tensed. 'I don't *have* to do anything, Jake.'

'It's common sense. You can't study and do a job if you're pregnant. You mustn't take risks.'

'Fine. I'll be careful.'

'But not with any help from me, eh? Well, that tells me all I need to know.'

'I don't know what you mean by that—'

'You know exactly what I mean.'

'Jake, understand this: nothing has changed between us. I am having a baby. *I am*, not *we are*.'

She thought he became a little paler, but he spoke calmly. 'You've already made that quite clear. But I told you before that I owe you, and I'd like to help.'

She didn't answer, but crossed her arms and looked mulish. It was Jake's turn to grow annoyed.

'And what about when the baby's born? Have you thought of that, you mad woman? You can't support yourself. You *have* to let me support you.'

'I don't have to do anything,' she said through gritted teeth.

'That's just fine talk. In practical terms you do have to do what's best for your baby, and that isn't the way you're living now.'

'Will you stop giving me orders? You can't do that any more.'

'I never gave you orders.'

'Oh, sure!'

'I never did,' he yelled.

'Of course not. Why bother giving orders to someone who scurries to do whatever you want without waiting to be asked?'

He stared. 'You make me sound like a bully.'

'No, you weren't,' she conceded with a sigh. 'You just never thought. And that's as much my fault as yours because I never forced you to think. I always gave in too easily.'

'And you're doing it again,' he pointed out.

'How do you mean?'

'Rushing to take the blame, like that. You shouldn't do it.'

'Right.'

'You should stand up to me.'

'Yes.'

'Don't let me be so overbearing.'

'I won't.'

'Except now, because I happen to be right.'

Kelly sighed and threw up her hands at this inevitable end. 'That's for me to decide,' she declared.

'So what are you going to do for money? Or are you planning something really stupid like leaving college?'

'I don't know,' she yelled back. 'I'll find another way of making money.'

'How?' he demanded remorselessly.

'Put a lodger in my spare room. I don't know. I'll think of something. But I'll tell you this, Jake. I won't be asking you for permission.'

'Kelly, will you see sense?' he roared.

'I have seen sense. I saw sense the day I booted you out.'

'Don't be so—where are you going? Come back here. *Kelly!*'

Dr Ainsley caught up with her in the café a few minutes later.

'Well done,' he said. 'That was the best entertainment we've had for a long time.'

'I suppose everyone heard every word.'

'Well, neither of you bothered to lower your voices.

Great stuff. And you did my patient a world of good. I haven't seen him so lively since he came in here.'

'We were arguing about my pregnancy. You didn't—?'

'Not guilty. I was pretty sure he'd spotted it for himself by the way he was looking at you when you turned green.'

'At exactly three o'clock in the afternoon. Just like last time, apparently.'

'He remembered that?'

'Jake always says his mind is like flypaper. Things stick to it for ages. It's very useful for a journalist.'

'Ah, yes. That must be it.' A figure appeared at the entrance of the café. 'Look who's here.' He raised his voice. 'Well done, Jake. And you're barely out of breath.'

He shifted for Jake to seat himself opposite Kelly, but then settled down again in his own seat.

'I'll stick around as referee,' he said. 'Retire to your opposite corners and when I say so, come out chucking cream buns.'

'That's all the cream buns in this place are good for,' Jake observed. 'Kelly, after you dashed off I realised that you'd been brilliant.'

She'd recovered her temper enough to smile. 'If you'd realised that years ago I might never have thrown you out.'

'May you be forgiven! I walked out.'

'Seconds ahead of getting my toe in your rear.'

'End of Round One,' Dr Ainsley declared. 'Kelly gets it on points.'

'She can have Round Two as well, since she came up with the perfect answer,' Jake said.

'So tell me how I was brilliant.'

'You said you'd take a paying lodger.'

'So?'

'Meet your first lodger. I'll need somewhere to crash when I get out of here, and with my rent you'll be able to leave that crummy job and—don't shake your head like that. It makes sense.'

'Nothing you've ever said has made sense, and the idea of us stuck under the same roof again when we've only just escaped each other—get real!'

'I think the two of you are overlooking something,' Dr Ainsley ventured.

They both turned to him. 'What?'

'Henry VIII.'

'Ignore him,' Jake advised, seeing Kelly's expression. 'He's been breathing in too much anaesthetic.'

'Henry VIII and Anne of Cleves,' Dr Ainsley went on. 'She was his fourth wife. They had an amicable divorce and stayed the best of buddies. She had the semi-official title of "The King's Dear Sister". You two have eight years behind you. I'm not talking about love, I'm talking about understanding, knowing how each other's minds work. Whether you like it or not, you're intertwined, connected—as in "three o'clock in the afternoon". What's funny?' Kelly was choking with laughter.

'I'm sorry, it's just the thought of him as Henry VIII. Mind you, he may not have the figure but he's sure got the attitude.'

'I'll be the perfect lodger,' he vowed.

'I'm sure you will, but not for me. Listen, you two, it's a lovely idea, but no.'

'Kelly!' They said it together.

'You've got windmills in your head. Both of you. And now I really am going before I get them too.'

That night her stint at the café seemed harder than ever. The afternoon had left her unsettled and now the smell of greasy food made her feel ill. An unwritten essay loomed before her like a barrier, and when she sat down to it the blank page danced before her eyes. She knew now that she must give up that job. She'd been right about taking a lodger. But not Jake. Anyone but Jake.

It was several days before she returned to the hospital, meaning this to be the last visit. She would confirm her refusal, say goodbye, and that would be that. She recalled another time, only recently, when she'd planned much the same thing and it hadn't gone that way. But this time it would be different.

Dr Ainsley intercepted her and took her to his room.

'There's something you should know,' he said hurriedly. 'The day before yesterday Jake discharged himself. He was so determined to get out that he just upped sticks and went.'

'And you let him?'

'I couldn't stop him. This isn't a gaol.'

'But why didn't you call me?'

'Because I don't have your number. You're not down as his next of kin. Nobody is. He went back to wherever he calls home, and that night one of his neighbours heard him groaning and called an ambulance. It wasn't very bad, and he's OK now. But if he's that determined to get out of here, he may do it again.'

'But surely he still needs nursing?'

'Yes, but not intensive nursing. Just rest and feeding, with a nurse calling in every day to see to the medical side. If he had anyone living with him I'd send him home to them like a shot, but he hasn't. And he has no family, as you told me. Oddly, for such a popular man, he's very much alone.'

Jake was back in bed, looking as though his escape and return to captivity had exhausted him. Kelly didn't speak at first, but went and sat beside him, his hand in hers.

After a while he said, 'I've been an idiot.'

'No change there, then,' she said, trying to keep her voice steady. The sight of him looking pale and defeated made her heart ache. 'Whatever possessed you to do such a daft thing?'

He shrugged. 'I was going stir crazy. You know me better than anyone. Can you imagine me settling in here? I know you want to see the back of me, and I don't blame you. It's just that all that brother and sister stuff the doc was handing out sounded pretty good for a while. But you were right to say no. If it doesn't work for you, it doesn't work.'

She could feel herself teetering on the edge of giving in, and made a last desperate attempt to fend off disaster. 'Olympia's really the right person to be looking after you, Jake.'

'She's out networking from dawn to dusk. Besides, I haven't got enough energy for Olympia just now.'

'Well, I don't suppose she'll be expecting you to— I mean, for a while—'

'Oddly enough, I didn't mean that. I meant the whole romantic thing. It makes me feel tired just to think of it.'

'Jake Lindley, whose appearance on the box is enough to make strong women swoon?' she teased.

'Yeah, right,' he agreed without enthusiasm.

'Oh Jake,' she sighed, 'what am I going to do?'

'Whatever you want. It's your call.'

She gave a snort of indignation. 'Oh, *please*! You must think I have a short memory. That was what you always said when you'd just tricked me into giving you your own way.'

'No change there, then,' he said, echoing her.

'But it doesn't work any more. Besides, you saw my spare room. It isn't even furnished.'

'I've thought of that.' He reached into his bedside cabinet and pulled out a slip of paper, which he put into her hand. 'This should cover furniture and paying workmen to install everything for you. You mustn't try to do any of it yourself.'

The amount of the cheque shocked her. 'But this is far more than it'll take to—'

'Put it to the first month's rent, then.' He made a sudden grimace, as if in pain. 'Let me do something for you, Kelly. Let me give as well as take.' When she was still silent he said huskily, 'Please.'

It wasn't Jake's way to say please. Whatever he wanted he charmed people into offering. She told herself it was a trick to fool her. But, looking into his eyes, she saw an anxiety that she'd never seen before, and heard again Dr Ainsley saying, 'For such a popular man, he's very much alone.'

'All right,' she said slowly. 'Just until you get back on your feet.'

'You mean, get back on my feet without falling straight off them?' he quipped.

'Until you're better, you can be my lodger.'

'No, I'll be your brother. Now, let's be practical. Have you given in your notice at that café?'

'No, but—'

He lifted the phone. 'Do it now.'

It took precisely five minutes to free her from the

café, partly because the boss was glad to be rid of her. She was a good employee, but his niece needed a job. He let this fact slip, making Kelly wonder just how long she would have been employed there anyway. It was almost enough to make a person believe in fate.

But she couldn't see Jake as fate. Jake was Henry VIII.

On second thoughts, forget Henry VIII. He was the devil. But the devil with charm.

CHAPTER SIX

IT WAS another week before Jake had recovered from his escape sufficiently to be allowed out of the hospital. In that time Kelly had his room furnished and redecorated by experts. It made quite a hole in the cheque, but still left her enough to ease her money concerns. When she tried to thank him he changed the subject.

'All right, let's be practical,' she said. 'You'll need some more clothes. If you'll give me your key I'll collect some for you.'

'Thanks, but there's no need,' he said quickly.

'I don't mind.' After their separation they had both vacated their old home, and secretly she was curious to see Jake's new apartment. 'Give me the key.'

'You don't have to bother,' he said stiffly. 'I've arranged all that.'

She suddenly felt very foolish. Of course Olympia would have done it for him. She probably had the key anyway. How could she have forgotten the real situation?

She made an excuse to leave, and bid him a bright, edgy goodbye.

The evening before he was due she concentrated hard on the chapter of a book she'd been set to read, knowing that her time would be much taken up next day. When her doorbell rang she didn't hear it the first time. At last she answered it and found Olympia standing outside. As always she looked glorious, her mane of blonde hair tousled to perfection. Her gracious smile

widened when she saw Kelly, and she enveloped her
in a scented embrace that almost made her gag.

'Kelly, *dear*, you don't mind my dropping in, do
you?'

'Not at all,' Kelly lied.

'I was so glad to hear that you'd been helping Jake.
It's so wonderful the way all his old friends have remembered him. I suppose we should call you an old
friend now, shouldn't we?'

'Not as old as some,' Kelly observed with a touch
of pardonable malice. Olympia had a good five years
over her.

She would have liked to throw this smiling woman
out, but somehow Olympia was inside the apartment,
looking it over as though she owned it, and throwing
open the door to the room that was to be Jake's.

'Very nice,' she said in a neutral voice. 'Although I
must say I'm a little surprised—well, no matter.'

'You mean you're surprised that Jake wanted to stay
with me?' Kelly asked coolly.

'If you like to put it that way. I don't think anything
about the present position is exactly what Jake would
have chosen, but let's not split hairs. We know how he
hates to hurt people's feelings.'

'He does if he thinks about it,' Kelly observed with
gentle irony. 'Jake's kind-hearted and he means well,
but mostly people's feelings are things he stubs his toe
on, and says sorry without really understanding what
the fuss was about. You'll find that out eventually.'

Olympia gave a tolerant smile. 'Perhaps he's like
that with some people, but I—well, you don't want to
hear about that.'

'No, I don't,' Kelly retorted with spirit. 'Because if

you're saying what I think you are, I wouldn't believe it. You have to take him as he is. He doesn't change.'

Olympia gave the hint of a simper. 'But a man does change—when he's in love.'

'Oh, cut it out, Olympia,' Kelly said, exasperated. 'You're not playing to camera now.' She spoke sharply to cover the little pain this glamorous woman's words gave her.

Olympia descended from her pedestal. 'Then, in plain words, it's no use clinging to the past. I'm sorry, Kelly, dear. But the truth is the truth, even when it hurts.'

'You seem to forget that *I* divorced *him*,' Kelly said crisply.

'But of course. Nothing else would have been dignified after he'd shown so clearly that he loved someone else.'

'Which you denied.'

'Certainly I denied it. Neither Jake nor I wanted my name bandied about. But the truth is the truth, whatever clever fictions he invented to protect me. Let him go, Kelly. We both know your marriage ended because he wanted to move on.'

Kelly drew a sharp breath. Out of the turmoil of bitter emotion only one thought was clear. Thank goodness she hadn't told Jake her baby was his.

'You won't mind if I come to see him?' Olympia continued sweetly. 'Or, once you've got him here—' her voice became teasingly theatrical '—are you going to bar the door and patrol the perimeter fence with dogs?'

'The only dog in the building is my neighbour's poodle, and he's fifteen and spends most of his time asleep,' Kelly said, refusing to be provoked. 'Come any time you like, stay as long as you like, just try not to disturb me when I'm working.'

'Ah, yes, you've gone back to school,' Olympia said, wisely not rising to the bait.

'College,' Kelly said. 'I'm taking a degree.'

'Jake told me all about it. There are so many varied courses on offer these days, aren't there? You can even get a degree in soap operas, I believe.'

'I wouldn't know. I'm studying archaeology, and just now I'm reading a particularly interesting book on ancient burial practices. There was this king who used to dispose of his surplus concubines by drugging their wine. They passed out, and when they awoke they were swathed in burial bandages and lying in a sarcophagus in a chamber deep underground. Apparently their cries used to echo for a week before they finally died into silence. I think it was a very ingenious way of getting rid of people. Can I offer you a glass of wine?'

Olympia declined, made her excuses and left.

Carl had agreed that she could skip his final lecture the following afternoon, to be at home for Jake's arrival.

'I'll give you the notes, and we'll have lunch in a day or so to chat about them,' he said easily. But then his face became concerned. 'Kelly, are you sure you're up to looking after a sick man in your condition?'

'Does the whole world know?' she demanded, aghast. 'I haven't told anyone.'

'The others won't have noticed, but I have a sixth sense. Actually a seventh sense. I'm the third of seven children. All through my childhood my mother was having babies, and by the time I was seventeen my two elder sisters had married and gone into production. By then I was an experienced baby-sitter so they hired me. That's how I earned money to take out girls.'

'Too many girls, according to Marianne,' Kelly said, smiling.

He grinned. 'All those babies have marked me for life. I love them, and I'm great with them, if I say it myself. So—' he took her hand and spoke solemnly '—if there's anything you want to know, my dear, just call on Uncle Carl. Seriously—' he reverted to normal '—if you need time off, trust me to understand.'

'Thanks, but this time off is to see Jake settled. I'm hoping not to take any for myself. I'm not going to let this pregnancy make any difference to my normal life. Now what?'

Carl had let out a hoot of laughter. 'Not make any difference? Oh, boy, have you got a lot to learn! Get out of here, and take as long as you need.'

On the day of Jake's arrival Kelly was home by mid-afternoon, a little breathless from climbing stairs as the building's lift was under repair. The phone rang as soon as she entered. It was Dr Ainsley.

'The ambulance has just left,' he said, 'so Jake will be with you any minute.'

'Actually, I'm a bit worried. The lift's broken down and I'm three floors up.'

'No sweat. The paramedics will bring him up in a wheelchair. I just called to warn you about what could be lying in wait. It wouldn't surprise me if he went into a deep depression quite soon.'

'But I thought that had already happened.'

'Kelly, I have to tell you—you ain't seen nothin' yet. The way he's been isn't so much depression as shock, and the fact that he's miserable in the hospital. Being in home surroundings will do him a world of good. He'll perk up, and you'll think everything's fine. So will he. That's the moment of danger. If I've judged him right it'll hit without warning, and he'll need you as never before.'

'As never before is right,' she said wryly. 'He never really has needed me, or anyone. And you're wrong about Jake. He's a very strong-minded person.'

'They're the worst,' Dr Ainsley told her, and hung up.

She had a cup of tea and tried to think logically. In a few minutes she would be sharing a home with Jake, while carrying his child. To all appearances their divorce had never happened.

That was what she had to fight, and she must do it by keeping her thoughts clear. She was not a wife, but a divorcée, a free woman, answerable to no man. The baby was off limits, and she was no longer in love with Jake. The slightly heightened heartbeat that she could sense was apprehension about what lay ahead.

She wondered how they would greet each other when he arrived. It would set the tone for the future, so, *Hello, darling,* was out. *Nice to see you,* didn't sound quite right somehow.

Glancing out of the window, she saw that the ambulance had just drawn up. A last quick check of Jake's room showed that everything was in place. By now they would have hauled a wheelchair up the stairs and she began to listen for the doorbell.

But it didn't ring.

Looking out again, she saw the ambulance still there, but no sign of the occupants. Puzzled, she opened her front door just in time to see Jake turning the corner to begin slowly climbing the last flight of stairs on his own two feet. Behind him were a male and a female paramedic, making frustrated efforts to help him and being firmly snubbed.

'I can manage,' Jake growled. 'Don't either of you dare touch me.'

Kelly had tried to plan her greeting, but at the sight of him driving himself on, perspiration streaming down his deadly pale face, all her calculations went out of her head and she yelled, *'Do you have no common sense?'*

'None at all,' he gasped. 'Never did have. Don't you know that by now?'

'I do but I tried to forget it. Silly me! Where's your wheelchair?'

The female paramedic was holding it. 'Here. But he won't let us use it.'

'Yes, he will,' Kelly said grimly.

'No, he won't,' Jake grated, reaching the top stair. 'You see? I told you I was fine.'

'You're not fine,' she raged. 'You're soft in the head. It would serve you right if you ended up back in hospital.'

'No way!' said the female paramedic with feeling. 'Now we've got rid of him, we're staying rid.'

'I once thought the same,' Kelly muttered. 'It's not that easy.'

At last they were gone and she could confront Jake, who'd made it to the sofa and was looking at her with the wry, sheepish expectancy that she knew of old. It meant he'd done something thoroughly insane and was hoping to buy his way out of it with charm.

Well, not this time, buster!

'It's a pity they won't take you back,' she snapped, 'because if they'd have you, I'd send you. You had to be a show-off, didn't you? You had to be clever. You had to be "Jake Lindley who's never fazed by anything".'

'I just wanted to prove I could make it alone.'

'Well, you couldn't, so what have you proved? Only that you're an idiot, and I knew that already.' Now the dam had broken there was no stopping her. Words poured out as the feelings of outrage swept her along.

'C'mon, Kelly,' he said at last. 'I know I shouldn't have done it, but—'

'No buts. I'm fed up with your buts. You shouldn't have done it, but, no, it's not good enough for you to be like anyone else. Big, glamorous TV image, but behind it there's just a bird-brained adolescent. You ought to be shot.'

As soon as the words were out she clutched her hair, horrified at herself. She'd said it often in the past, half laughing, and he'd laughed back. But she wished she'd bitten her tongue out before she'd said it now.

'I thought I had been,' Jake said wryly.

'Oh, no, Jake, I didn't mean that. It just—I don't know—'

'It's all right. You weren't thinking. Welcome to the club.' He managed a frayed grin.

'Oh, heavens!' she said wretchedly. 'It was a dreadful thing to say, wasn't it?'

'It was so dreadful it was entertaining. I'd laugh if I dared. Will you please forget it?'

'Thanks,' she said, sincerely grateful for his understanding. 'Now go to bed and let me atone by a bit of fussing. Or are you too macho to admit you need to lie down?'

'Nope.'

She took his bag into the bedroom and he followed,

sitting down on the bed and taking her hand in his thin one.

'I'm sorry, Kelly,' he said, speaking seriously. 'If you think I'll be too much trouble I'll go back to the hospital.'

'Hah! As if! You heard what that paramedic said. You can stay here but you have to behave yourself.'

'Yes, ma'am!' he said meekly. He dropped her hand, since she didn't seem to notice that he was holding it.

'Let me unpack for you.'

'Thanks, but that's something I really can manage for myself without collapsing. I don't want to be more trouble to you than I have to be.'

'Fine.'

She got out of the room quickly to hide the fact that she wanted to cry.

For a while she saw little of Jake. He slept long hours and was often only just awakening as Kelly left for her classes. At first she would make him some tea before leaving, but he discouraged her, insisting that he could do this much for himself.

Kelly was there for the first visit of the district nurse, a pleasant middle-aged woman called Emily, who changed Jake's dressing, checked that he was taking his medication, made him comfortable, and stayed for a coffee and chat. She confirmed that he'd taken no real hurt from climbing the stairs.

'He just overtaxed his strength, but he'll make that up now.'

'Is that why he's sleeping so much? He seemed much livelier in the hospital.'

'Partly that,' Emily agreed. 'Also he strikes me as a

man who's been on pins for some time. Now he feels more able to relax.'

Kelly gave her a key to the front door, in case Jake should be dead to the world next time. In fact he usually was, and for a while it seemed Emily saw more of him than Kelly did herself. Gradually he grew more wakeful. In the evening they would eat together, but he would return to his room immediately afterwards, and she had the feeling he was deliberately keeping out of her way.

She soon learned that her financial calculations were way out. Without Jake's money she couldn't have managed. They never spoke of this, but she knew he sensed it, and straight away embarked on a campaign to make her accept more. The battle was unspoken, but real, and since Jake was a canny fighter he won almost every round.

He'd never been the most alert of men when her needs and feelings were concerned, but now he seemed to have an extra sense that enabled him to head her off at the pass. She came home one day to find her kitchen adorned by an expensive, top-of-the-range microwave. He'd bought it over the phone and it had been delivered that afternoon.

He explained that since living alone he'd become used to microwaving his own food, and now there were several dishes that would be easy on his injured stomach and could be cooked this way. Soon Kelly had fallen in love with the machine. It reduced her cooking time to a minimum, made her crowded life manageable and, above all, it didn't smell of grease.

Round One to Jake.

Round Two started with a visit from Olympia. She gave Kelly the barest greeting that courtesy demanded before vanishing into Jake's room for the rest of the evening. When she emerged he was already asleep. Olympia gave Kelly a little lecture on not disturbing him and made a tinkling remark about 'poor Jake' being confined in 'that little rabbit hutch'.

Kelly suppressed her rage until he'd been collected by ambulance next morning for his hospital check-up, then stormed into action. By the time he returned his things were in her bedroom and she had moved into the little room. When he tried to protest she silenced him with a look.

He retaliated by doubling the rent he paid her, sending the cheque directly to her bank account and getting Emily to mail it, so that she knew nothing for several days. Since she'd been overdrawn at the time she had no choice but to accept.

Round Two to Jake.

There were arguments on these occasions, but that was OK. Arguments she could cope with. It was when the surface was smooth that she floundered.

Superficially they'd settled easily into their strange life. Their conversations were friendly, yet each one was an individual effort, as though the ground rules had to be renegotiated every time. And that was true because they'd somehow never discovered the right tone of voice to govern their life. Without it, they couldn't relax.

Their row on the first day had got them off to a good start, breaking the ice. Yet they hadn't managed to build on it. Kelly didn't want to bicker with him lest she say something else that was unforgivable. Jake seemed to have forgiven and forgotten, but she still blamed herself. That left only cautious politeness, which was terrible.

The solution to this awkwardness turned out to be sexual fantasies. Wild, exotic, uninhibited, mind-blowing sexual fantasies: mental orgies of erotica.

Not Kelly's. The fight to keep her stomach settled was becoming the centre of her life. Her fantasies concerned hot, sweet tea and dry biscuits. Sex was the last thing on her mind.

But for Jake's female fans it was different. Ever since his handsome face, shaggy, wind-blown hair and hard, lean body had first appeared on screen he'd received a stream of letters from hot-blooded ladies containing explicit invitations. It was a phenomenon Kelly had heard of before, and she knew in her heart that it meant nothing. Yet as a young wife, haunted by her failure to produce a child and uncertain of her husband's love, she'd hated it. Jake had tried to share the joke with her, and been baffled that she didn't find it funny.

'It's not the real me,' he'd tried to explain. 'I'm a disembodied face and they project their imaginations on it. I don't meet them and I don't want to. Darling, you're creating a storm in a teacup.'

'I suppose I am,' she'd said, anxious to not bore him by making a fuss.

He'd smiled and patted her on the shoulder, evidently relieved that she was starting to be reasonable. But then he'd been unwise enough to add, 'Anyway, mine are pretty restrained. You should see some of the—' He broke off belatedly realising that this wasn't the cleverest thing to say.

'So you all sit around swapping notes,' she'd accused.

'Don't make a big deal of something that doesn't matter.' Trying to be funny, he'd managed to miss his footing again. 'Look, why don't you answer them for me? Tell them I'm not available because you keep me on a ball and chain.'

That little gem had sparked a row that lasted half the night. As he'd grown exasperated, she'd grown scared. At last he'd said, 'I'd better go out for a while, because everything I say just seems to make it worse.'

They'd never discussed it again. She'd suppressed her feelings for fear of irritating him, as she'd done so often over the years.

Now he was passing the time trying to answer some of the correspondence that had flooded him ever since the shooting. Kelly sensed that it was causing him problems, but didn't particularly think about it until one evening when Jake was in the kitchen and she happened to notice a black lace bra falling out of an envelope on the table.

There was no jolt of anguish, such as she would once have known. Instead she felt only intrigued as she held it up. That was when he appeared in the doorway.

'She's a big girl, isn't she?' she said, considering the size.

'I suppose so.' He was regarding her cautiously.

Kelly glanced over the letter. 'She wants you to do *what*?' she asked, wide-eyed. 'Oh, my, my! You *are* going to have a heavy schedule!'

'Cut it out, will you? And who said you could read that?'

'I just wondered why you were making such heavy weather of your fan mail. You've always taken fans in your stride. You smile and make jokes, and they go away thinking how charming and unspoilt you are.'

'I'll thank you to keep your sarcasm to yourself, ma'am. This kind of fan I couldn't cope with.'

'If you've made the tea why don't you pour me a nice big cup while I get reading?'

'No way! I remember the grief you used to give me about them.'

'I used to make a fuss about a lot of silly things.'

He returned with two mugs of tea to find her sitting at the table, deep in pink scented pages. His sense of humour was reviving as it dawned on him that she wasn't upset.

'You'd hardly believe what turns that lady on,' he said, indicating the pink letter.

'Evidently *you* turn her on,' Kelly mused.

'But only in certain circumstances.' He pointed to some lines on the page. 'I don't think we even have any peanut butter, do we?'

Kelly's lips twitched. 'She was probably planning to supply her own. Mind you, I'll buy some straight away if it'll help your recovery.'

'Nothing these women want of me would help my recovery,' he said, sounding harassed. 'More likely to lay me flat on my back—'

'Not "Passionate of Kensington,"' she said, riveted by another letter. 'The last place she wants you is on your back. In fact—'

'Yes, I've read that one, thank you,' he said, hastily snatching it from her. 'She has a vivid imagination. I don't think what she suggests is even physically possible.'

'Not in your present condition, but after a few months' weight training I should think you could accommodate her,' Kelly said wickedly.

'Get lost!' He ran his hand distractedly through his hair. 'It's worse than last time.'

'I suppose the fantasy is more exciting with a hero,' she mused. 'How do you answer them?'

'With great difficulty,' he growled.

'Yes, I can see the problem. "Dear Madam, in reply to yours of the thirteenth inst. I have to report your suggestion impractical, owing to high price of peanut butter."'

'You're finding this very funny, aren't you?' he said coldly.

'I think it's hilarious. You, a sex god!'

'You won't think it's so funny when hundreds of rampaging women turn up here demanding my body.'

'No problem. I'll just tell them about your knock knees.'

'I do not have knock knees.'

'Ho, ho, ho!'

'What do you mean, "ho, ho, ho!"? I do not have knock knees.'

'They're like a pair of castanets, your knees.'

'May you be forgiven!'

This was better, she thought, remembering his silent despair when she'd first been to the hospital. Now he was glaring, animated, giving as good as he got. Another turn of the screw wouldn't hurt.

'All right,' she said in a tone of concession. 'I take it back. Your knees aren't big.'

'Thank you.'

'It's your legs that are skinny.'

'There is nothing the matter with my legs.'

'Oh, yeah? Why do you never appear on camera in shorts when you're in a hot country? Because you know that the dreadful sight would reduce your fan club to one short-sighted little old lady. With or without fantasies. What does Olympia say?'

'I do not discuss my knees with Olympia,' he said through gritted teeth.

'Why? Did they put her off?'

'Of course not.'

'But she has seen them?'

'Yes.'

'And she didn't say anything?'

'No.'

'Probably the first kind thing she's ever done.'

But he'd caught up with her dancing wits now and was regarding her with wry affection. 'The hell with you!' he said with a grin.

'Really?'

'Think I can't see through you?'

'It took you long enough,' she jeered.

It was on the tip of his tongue to say he'd never seen her in this mood, but he changed his mind and announced he was going to bed.

He returned a few minutes later to collect his correspondence with as much dignity as he could manage, and after a brief tussle managed to prise the scented letter from her grasp.

'Actually, Jake, it's fascinating,' she said, following him to the door, which he shut in her face.

'I'm glad I'm contributing to your entertainment,' he yelled through the door.

'No, I mean it's a sociological phenomenon. Carl's into sociology, he'd love to investigate this. I don't think he's ever met anyone it's actually happened to before.'

The door opened.

'If,' Jake said, speaking emphatically, 'you repeat a word of this to Carl or anyone else, that day will be your last on earth.'

'But his interest would be purely scientific,' she said innocently.

'Rubbish! His interest would be in making me a laughing stock. Now, you promise me—'

'All right,' she sighed. 'Spoilsport!'

'Do you mind leaving?'

But she had a parting shot. 'Pity. It would have made a great thesis.'

'Kelly, I'm warning you—'

'Oh, go to bed!'

That was the end of the matter, for the moment. But the next morning she had the satisfaction of coming across him in a bath robe, studying his legs in the mirror, a frown creasing his forehead.

'Checking your assets?' she teased.

'Checking the facts. And there is nothing wrong with my knees.'

'Of course not. They're splendid knees. I've always liked them.'

'But you said—'

She gave him her sweetest smile. 'I'm a liar.'

CHAPTER SEVEN

CARL had spoken truly when he called himself an expert on pregnancy and babies. At college he would often join Kelly for lunch and observe her intake with an experienced eye, sometimes advising her to 'eat more fibre'. They had long talks about her condition, heads close together in their enthusiasm, and Kelly realised that the college was speculating about them, for Carl had devastating film-star looks. But he was merely showing her the kindness and support of a brother, and she valued him for that.

Occasionally he would drive her home, carrying her books up and coming in for tea. Sometimes Jake would join them, but more often he would retreat to his room. And he never, ever mentioned Carl when he and Kelly were alone.

Another thought that neither of them voiced was that Kelly's pregnancy was well into its fourth month, nearing the time when she'd lost the last baby. As the weeks passed the silence seemed to grow more deafening. Sometimes, she thought, it was like living with an extra presence that had parked itself in the centre of the apartment. They dodged around it, and otherwise pretended not to know it was there.

Her first thought, on waking, was to listen to her body, checking for any unusual twinge. Only when she felt nothing wrong could she relax and start the day.

Jake's health too was giving cause for cheer. As his strength returned he began to venture out to the local shops, or he would stroll in the little park close to Kelly's apartment. Now and then she came with him, and they would walk together, arms linked, but saying little. Kelly always thought of herself as supporting Jake, and it amused her one evening to discover that he thought of himself as the support.

'It's going to be a while before I need propping up,' she laughed, settling on a park bench.

'Just taking care.'

'I'm feeling very well. And I'm not worried, honestly.'

After a moment he said, 'You're lying. You're scared.'

'How do you know?'

'Because you're not knitting things. Last time you started knitting from the first day. The place was awash with needles and patterns.'

She smiled. 'You used to say you couldn't move without tangling your feet in white wool.'

'Yes, but I liked it too. And all the soft toys you bought. I'll never forget the day you finished your first pair of bootees. You were so proud.'

'Until I discovered that I'd gone cross-eyed on the pattern and made the second one two sizes larger than the first.'

'Then you burst into tears and couldn't stop for hours. I didn't know what to do.'

'You were very practical,' she remembered. 'You said all I had to do was knit two more the same, put the two small ones together as the first pair, and keep the other pair for later. It was a very good suggestion. I don't know what made me thump you with that toy giraffe.'

'You didn't.'

'I did.'

'You did *not* thump me with a toy giraffe,' Jake said firmly.

'Jake, I clearly remember—'

'It was a toy elephant. His name was Dolph, short for Dolphin.'

'Why did we call him Dolphin?'

'Because he was an elephant,' Jake explained patiently.

'Well, I guess that figures. But I'm sure a giraffe came into it somewhere.'

'Now you're just confusing things,' he said severely. 'It was definitely Dolph the elephant. I know because I—because its trunk was always wonky after that.'

She barely registered his verbal stumble as they laughed together. Then Kelly said firmly, 'It'll be all right this time. Carl says one of his sisters miscarried the first time, then went on to have three healthy babies.'

His smile faded. 'You talk to Carl about this?'

Something tense in his voice made her bristle. 'Any reason why not?'

'No, no,' he said quickly. 'It just seems odd, talking babies with your professor.'

She would have explained about Carl's family and all his baby sitting experience, but Jake suddenly said, 'Maybe it's time we went home.' And the moment was gone.

One day Kelly arrived home early from college. Jake was in his room, but appeared as soon as he heard her. 'Are you all right?' he asked quickly.

'I'm fine.'

'Are you sure?'

The Harlequin Reader Service® — Here's how it works:

Accepting your 2 free books and gift places you under no obligation to buy anything. You may keep the books and gift and return the shipping statement marked "cancel." If you do not cancel, about a month later we'll send you 6 additional books and bill you just $3.34 each in the U.S., or $3.80 each in Canada, plus 25¢ shipping & handling per book and applicable taxes if any.* That's the complete price and — compared to cover prices of $3.99 each in the U.S. and $4.50 each in Canada — it's quite a bargain! You may cancel at any time, but if you choose to continue, every month we'll send you 6 more books, which you may either purchase at the discount price or return to us and cancel your subscription.

*Terms and prices subject to change without notice. Sales tax applicable in N.Y. Canadian residents will be charged applicable provincial taxes and GST.

If offer card is missing write to: Harlequin Reader Service, 3010 Walden Ave., P.O. Box 1867, Buffalo NY 14240-1867

NO POSTAGE
NECESSARY
IF MAILED
IN THE
UNITED STATES

BUSINESS REPLY MAIL
FIRST-CLASS MAIL   PERMIT NO. 717-003   BUFFALO, NY

POSTAGE WILL BE PAID BY ADDRESSEE

HARLEQUIN READER SERVICE
3010 WALDEN AVE
PO BOX 1867
BUFFALO NY 14240-9952

GET FREE BOOKS and a FREE GIFT WHEN YOU PLAY THE...

SLOT MACHINE GAME!

Just scratch off the silver box with a coin. Then check below to see the gifts you get!

YES! I have scratched off the silver box. Please send me the 2 free Harlequin Romance® books and gift for which I qualify. I understand I am under no obligation to purchase any books, as explained on the back of this card.

386 HDL DRRJ

186 HDL DRRY
(H-RA-01/03)

Worth TWO FREE BOOKS plus a BONUS Mystery Gift!

Worth TWO FREE BOOKS!

Worth ONE FREE BOOK!

TRY AGAIN!

Visit us online at www.eHarlequin.com

DETACH AND MAIL CARD TODAY!

'Why shouldn't I be?'

'Because you're not usually home at this time?'

'There were no lectures for the rest of today.'

'And that's all?'

The worry on his face touched her. 'Jake, it's all right. There's no sign of a miscarriage.'

'But it would be about now, wouldn't it? After all—' Jake's words ran down. There was no way of asking exactly how pregnant she was. If the baby had been conceived on the night of the party, she was approaching the crucial time. By tortuous argument he'd half convinced himself that the child was his, but she had never confirmed it, and he was too proud to demand a straight answer.

She might already have been pregnant that night, and now be already past the danger point. But would she have allowed him into her bed if there was another man? He knew she'd changed, but that much? The thought gave him a strange pain over his heart.

'I wouldn't like you to suffer again,' he said harshly. 'That's all. No need to make a fuss about it.'

'No,' she agreed. 'I'm fine. Shall I get you something to eat?'

'I'll get it. Why don't you lie down for a while?'

'OK, I'll lie on the sofa for a few minutes. Thank you.'

It really was pleasant to stretch out and be waited on, although she was feeling well and strong. She closed her eyes and listened to the little sounds Jake made in the kitchen. She grew dozy, and was barely conscious of his muttered, 'Damn! No milk!', followed by the front door opening and closing. She might have completely sunk into sleep but for the shrilling of

Jake's mobile phone. Yawning, she answered it and found herself talking to Olympia.

'I'm afraid Jake isn't here at the moment,' she said pleasantly. 'Can I get him to call you back?'

'No need for that. Just to confirm about tonight, eight-thirty at my apartment. Can you remember that?'

'I'll try,' Kelly said humbly. 'If I have difficulty I could always write it down, couldn't I?'

Olympia snorted and hung up.

When Jake returned with milk a few moments later Kelly was at the table unpacking her books. 'Don't forget you have a date with Olympia tonight,' she said.

'Have I?'

'She called to remind you that it's eight-thirty at her apartment.'

Jake stared. 'I never made any arrangement with her for tonight.'

'Well, you seem to have one now.'

'You had no right to make a date for me,' he said, outraged.

'From the way she spoke I thought it was all fixed.' A tiny inspired devil made Kelly add, 'She was very concerned about your welfare. Kept asking me if you'd recovered all your strength yet.' She added casually, 'I told her I thought you probably had, although I couldn't swear to it.'

'You made that up.'

She looked at him. 'Sure of that?'

'Kelly, believe me I'll wring your neck one of these days.'

'What are you getting worked up about? It doesn't matter to me any more. We're both free agents.'

He resisted the temptation to burst out, *You're hav-*

*ing my baby. You ought to mind, not sit there calmly
making assignations for me!*

But he stayed silent. What could he say?

After a while he said grumpily, 'I'm not going out.
Something might happen.'

'Why should it? I've been well all day.'

'At college, surrounded by people to watch out for
you. I'm not leaving you alone.'

'You just did.'

'That was ten minutes to get some milk. I'm talking
about your being alone for hours.'

'You're being absurd, you know that?'

'I'm not going out!'

'All right, all right. You don't need to shout.'

'I do need to shout, Kelly, because if I don't shout
you don't hear.'

Her temper flared. 'That's rich, coming from the man
who turned creative deafness into an art.'

'I'm not arguing. I'll just call Olympia back and put
her off, and then the subject's closed.'

'Who says it's closed?' He didn't answer. *'Jake!'*

'I can't hear you. I've gone creatively deaf. Remember,
you're dealing with the man who turned it into an art.'

She fumed while he made the call. She wasn't sure
why she'd suddenly got mad. Perhaps she was trying
to deny the pleasure that had caught her off guard at
his protectiveness. Enough! It was too late for that.
Anger was safer.

Jake made an exasperated sound. 'She's turned her
mobile off,' he grunted. 'Never mind, she'll be at the
studio.' He called the studio and gave Olympia's name.

After an impatient pause he said, 'Do you know
where she went?—all right, if she calls in, ask her to

contact me urgently. Say there's a problem about to-night.'

'I wish you'd go,' Kelly said, following him into the kitchen. 'I've got an essay about ancient Egypt, and you'll be in the way.'

'I'll be as quiet as a mouse. Anyway, I can't go out now that I've cancelled.'

'You haven't cancelled. You never reached Olympia.'

'She'll understand as soon as she gets that message.'

'I don't think she *will* get it.'

'Nonsense. Why shouldn't she?'

Because she doesn't want to get it, Kelly thought, exasperated. Were all men this thick? *Why do you think she switched her mobile off?*

But she judged it wiser to stay silent. She could be wrong. Olympia might be an honest woman, sincerely in love with Jake, wanting only what was best for him.

And pigs might fly!

As the minutes slipped by he kept looking at his watch, growing impatient. The phone stayed silent.

'Go!' Kelly said at last. 'I have an essay to write, and you're driving me nuts.'

'I'm not doing anything.'

'You're hovering.'

'Well, pardon me for breathing.'

'I don't mind your breathing, it's your hovering I can't take. Now for pity's sake get dressed, go out, do whatever it takes to make Olympia happy.'

'That's a thoroughly immoral suggestion!'

'I meant buy her dinner,' Kelly said innocently.

'I'm not leaving you alone.'

'If I need company there's always Carl.'

Jake's eyes narrowed. 'Why Carl?'

'He's a good friend.'

'That wouldn't be why you want to get rid of me?'

She tore her hair. 'I want to get rid of you because you're acting like a broody hen! Now will you please keep quiet and leave me with Tutankhamun?'

'All right, all right. Don't get agitated, it's bad for the baby.'

For an hour there was peace of a kind. Jake never spoke, but she was aware of him rustling in the background. It was a relief when the telephone rang. Something about the shrill told Kelly that it was Olympia, and she wasn't pleased.

'I tried to get back to you,' Jake explained. 'I hoped you'd have my message that there was a problem about tonight... No, I'm not ill, it's Kelly...'

With a swift movement Kelly whisked the phone out of his hand. 'Olympia,' she said graciously, 'I'm sorry to have spoiled your evening. Why don't you come to my place? I'll be going out soon.'

'The hell you will!' Jake growled.

'The hell I won't!' she replied firmly.

'If Carl wants to see you he can come here.'

'What a great idea! Jake, you're a genius.'

'Are you still there?' came Olympia's chilly voice down the line. Being sidelined wasn't what she was used to.

'Of course,' Kelly told her. 'I'll tell Jake you're coming over. He's so looking forward to seeing you.' She hung up and immediately dialled Carl's number.

'You said I could talk to you whenever I wanted,' she reminded him.

In a few minutes he was on his way and Jake was fulminating.

'What's your game, Kelly?'

'I just thought you'd like a pleasant evening with your girlfriend.'

'Here? In a jolly foursome with you and Carl?'

'We'll go out and leave you two alone. Don't worry, I won't cramp your style.'

'Maybe I don't want you to leave me alone with Olympia.'

'Why? Have you quarrelled?'

'No, but—'

'I'm just trying to be a good friend.'

'Yeah,' he said grumpily. 'Sure.'

From there the evening went downhill. Olympia arrived half an hour later, done up to the nines. Kelly greeted her amiably before saying, 'You won't mind if I leave you? I have to work.' To Jake she mouthed, 'Take her out.'

'No,' he mouthed back.

Kelly groaned and vanished into her room.

Instantly Olympia's arms were around Jake's neck. 'I think you're a positive saint,' she murmured against his mouth.

He disengaged himself gently, with a significant glance at Kelly's door.

'You're right,' Olympia said with a sigh. 'My poor dear, it must be very hard for you.'

'It's harder for Kelly,' Jake said stubbornly. 'Fancy getting stuck with me again when she thought she was rid of me for good.'

Olympia's face showed what she thought of this, but she let the matter drop and instead began to question him about his health.

'I'm fine, I'm fine,' he said hastily. 'It's just that I don't seem able to get it all together. My stomach still reacts badly to some foods.'

What he didn't tell her was how he would awaken feeling full of beans and ready to return to normal life, only to find his strength draining away around noon. 'Like a bath when the plug's been pulled,' was how he'd expressed it to Kelly, but he said not a word to Olympia. She wasn't the sort of woman to whom a man could confide weakness.

With relief he managed to discourage her from this interrogation, but worse was to come. When Kelly emerged from her room Olympia started again on her, demanding full details of Jake's life and treatment. The subject of this concern became uneasy, then embarrassed, but Kelly answered everything serenely, even managing a laugh as she said, 'Please don't worry, Olympia. I promise you I'm taking good care of him. Anyone would think you were his mother, to be so concerned.'

Olympia was too wise to answer this, but Jake gave Kelly a quick, appraising glance.

The ring of the doorbell prevented matters getting any more awkward. Carl breezed in, impossibly handsome, smiling, pulling Kelly into his arms for a hug. Laughing, she hugged him back.

'Who's that?' Olympia muttered.

'That is Professor Carl Franton,' Jake muttered, emphasising 'Professor' edgily. 'From Kelly's college.'

'Is he the father of—?'

'Very possibly.'

'Then why—?'

'Not now, Olympia. I don't meddle with Kelly's private life.'

'But shouldn't he—?'

'I said *not now*.'

'All right. Let's talk about us and what we're going to do together. I have so many plans—'

Jake tried to concentrate on what she was saying, but it was hard when he was straining to hear the other two. Carl had brought a baby book with him, and he and Kelly were going through it together, exclaiming and laughing. But when Carl spoke seriously he lowered his voice, which struck Jake as a dirty trick.

'Jake.' Olympia touched his arm.

'I'm sorry?'

'I asked if you were thinking of new projects.'

'I've been working out ideas,' he said lamely.

Out of the corner of his eye he saw Kelly go into the kitchen, and he made an excuse to Olympia.

'What's up with you?' Kelly demanded as he appeared in the kitchen. 'You've been sitting there looking all struck of a heap. You can't treat Olympia like that. She's important to your career.'

'Well, maybe my career doesn't depend on her.'

'I just meant don't close off your options. Lighten up, Jake. We can't spend the whole evening like this.'

'May I remind you that this cosy little gathering was your idea? And not one of your better ones.'

'Stop getting agitated. It's not good for you.'

'And stop telling me what to do.'

'Just part of my duties.' She couldn't resist adding, 'I'm sure Anne of Cleves never had this much trouble with Henry VIII.'

'If she was anything like you I'm surprised he didn't behead her along with the others,' he snapped.

Kelly sniffed pathetically. 'That's a nice thing to say when I'm doing my best for you.'

'Hell, Kelly, it was only a joke! All right, it was a lousy one and I'm sorry. Don't cry—you're bound to be a bit sensitive just now—it's part of being pregnant, but I'm sorry.' Desperately he put his arms about her. 'Don't cry. Please, please don't cry.'

'Oh, get along with you, of course I'm not crying.'

'What?'

Her face was completely dry and her eyes full of mischief. 'Fooled you, though, didn't I?'

'Kelly, I swear I'll—'

'You'll what? Remember my delicate condition.'

He grinned reluctantly. 'You're the most maddening woman!'

'Tonight was a mistake,' she admitted. 'Why don't you suggest going out for a drink?'

'Great idea. Leave it to me.'

Carl, coming to find Kelly, was firmly detained in the doorway by Jake's hand. 'We're all going out for a drink,' he announced. 'I'm shut up here far too much. It'll do me good to get out.'

Olympia agreed to this with relief. Jake helped her on with her coat and had reached into the wardrobe's for Kelly's jacket before he realised that she was no longer with him.

Investigation revealed her to be still in the kitchen with Carl, deep in argument.

'No, no, you've got it all wrong,' Carl was saying. 'I keep telling you this in class but you never believe me. The pyramids—'

Jake coughed from the doorway. 'Are you two coming?' he asked coldly.

'Sure.' Carl beamed goodwill. 'You know, this wife of yours has gotten a bee in her bonnet—'

'She's not my wife,' Jake declared in a flat voice.

Carl beamed at Kelly. 'That's right, you're not,' he

said, with such a pleased inflection that Jake nearly knocked him down on the spot.

'Sorry,' Kelly said. 'When we get arguing we never know when to stop.'

'How delightful,' Olympia said, appearing beside Jake. 'How you must enjoy your talks! Why don't we go on ahead? You can join us when you've decided about the pyramids.'

'What a good idea!' Kelly exclaimed, with more eagerness than Jake thought was proper.

'Better if we all go together,' he tried to insist.

'But I'm not ready, and Carl wants a cup of tea first. You go on. We'll catch up.'

'We'll be in the Red Lion,' he growled.

He opened the door to Olympia with a gallant flourish and stood back to let her pass. He glanced back at Kelly and Carl, who were already sitting together on the sofa, riffling through a book. Nothing could have been more innocent, and nothing could have annoyed him more.

The Red Lion was a small pub two streets away. It was cheerful but slightly shabby, and not at all what Olympia was used to. Jake managed to find them a table in the corner, not too close to the piped music, which made her wince.

'Do you realise this is the first time we've been together outside that apartment?' she asked meltingly.

'What was that?' Jake cupped his ear.

She repeated the words, but at a volume that robbed them of their cooing quality and made them sound like a nag.

'What a delightful place this is,' she tried again. 'Not sophisticated but—full of character.'

'I never was sophisticated,' Jake said. 'In some of

the places I've knocked around this would be luxury. It suits me.'

'But don't you remember Paris—the night we had dinner together at that restaurant in the Eiffel Tower? That was a special time, wasn't it?'

He felt awkward. He'd felt awkward then, he remembered.

'And afterwards you came to my room,' she reminded him.

'And got too drunk to go through with it.'

'But I honoured you for that. You were a married man, and you took it seriously. But now—' She touched his hand and smiled into his eyes. 'Now it's different.'

'Yes, a lot of things are different,' he agreed sombrely, taking a surreptitious look at his watch. Where was Kelly?

A burst of loud music made Olympia wince. 'Do we have to stay here?' she said, looking around her with distaste. 'I'm sure there are nicer places.'

'I told Kelly we'd be here,' Jake said stubbornly. 'I don't want her to turn up and find us gone.'

'Oh, darling,' Olympia squeezed his hand. 'You don't really think they're coming, do you?'

'What do you mean?'

'Well—people can get very deeply involved in discussing—the pyramids. And let's face it, there's a lot they can't say with you around.'

'But it was Kelly who—' he stopped.

'Kelly who suggested the drink, and then backed out when you were committed?' Olympia asked quizzically.

'Yes, dammit!' he snapped.

'You can't really blame her. She's in a very equivocal position between you and Carl.'

'What do you mean, equivocal?'

'Well, why isn't she living with him? They're obviously very close, and you say he's the father—'

'I said he might be.'

'Are there any other candidates?'

Without warning a pit had appeared at his feet. Hell would freeze over before he admitted to Olympia that after backing away from her bed he'd slept with his ex-wife, possibly fathered her child, but didn't know because she was keeping him emotionally at arm's length.

'I told you once to leave this,' he said firmly. 'Kelly and I are like brother and sister. There are questions I don't ask her because the answers are none of my business.'

Like, did she fool me into going out so that she could be alone with Carl? A husband could ask, but how can I?

The conversation limped along for another half an hour before he could decently put her into a cab and bid her goodnight. Olympia kissed him tenderly, as if to say that she understood. He only wished he understood it himself.

The lights were on when he reached the apartment, but there was no sign of life. Then Jake heard the murmur of voices coming from behind Kelly's closed bedroom door. Kelly murmuring, Carl in response, then a soft, feminine laugh that made the hair stand up on the back of Jake's neck.

'That's lovely,' he heard her say. 'Oh, yes, I like that.'

Then Carl, 'As long as you're pleased, Kelly. That's the main thing. This is half the fun of parenthood.'

Jake stood very still, hoping for something more that would explain what he'd heard, but the voices dropped to murmurs. He waited there for a long while, before a sense that his behaviour was undignified drove him to bed. He lay listening for Carl's departure until, despite his determination not to, he fell asleep.

CHAPTER EIGHT

JAKE didn't know what made him awaken, but one moment he was asleep, and the next he was sitting up in bed, fully alert. Opening his door, he found the apartment silent and dark. Kelly's door was ajar and he ventured to push it gently and look in. The glow from the window showed him that the room was empty.

Flicking the light on he discovered that the bed hadn't been slept in. Spread over the duvet were books of nursery wallpaper, and pages of scrawled notes. But there was no sign of Kelly.

Some instinct made him go to the window. It overlooked the front, and the little park where they had talked the other night. There were still some park lights on, and he could just make out the tiny children's playground, with a couple of swings and one plain wooden carousel, aimlessly turning. After a moment he identified the person sitting on it. She had a forlorn aspect, huddled in a thick jacket, arms crossed over her chest against the night air, turning and turning aimlessly. In a minute Jake had thrown on some clothes and was hurrying downstairs.

By the time he neared the carousel it was moving very slowly, bringing Kelly face to face with him, then carrying her gently away again. She didn't seem surprised by his sudden appearance, and he wondered if she was even aware of him. He climbed on next to her.

Kelly didn't speak, but she smiled and tucked her hand into the crook of his arm.

'Well,' he said at last, 'did the two of you decide?'

'Decide?'

'How to decorate the baby's room. That's what you were mulling over, wasn't it?'

She gave a brief laugh. 'Yes. We can't decide between fluffy penguins and fluffy bears.'

He considered. 'I prefer fluffy tigers myself.'

'Uh-uh! Carl's determined on penguins.'

Jake made a face. 'Well, if that's what Carl wants... Is he planning to do the decorating as well?'

'He did mention it.'

'There's no need. I'm strong enough for a bit of painting.'

'No way,' she said at once. 'You're going to be on the sick list for a while yet. Leave it to Carl. Anyway, it can wait. There are still important matters to be agreed. If I give in about penguins on the walls I expect to choose the stencils on the furniture.'

If he'd really been her brother he could have asked which room she was planning to turn over to the baby. Probably the small one, where she was now sleeping. But that left her nowhere to go, except his room. Which meant that she was looking ahead to his departure.

Jake tried phrasing the question several ways before abandoning the attempt.

He pushed the ground with his foot, to speed up the carousel.

'There was one of these where we used to live,' he said after a while. 'Just after we were married.'

'I remember,' she said softly. 'I used to think I'd take our baby on it one day.'

He reached for her hand in his arm and gave it a squeeze.

Turn, turn…the park was gliding gradually around them.

'I'm sorry I wasn't there,' he said quietly.

He wondered if he should explain that he meant when she'd lost the baby, but she immediately picked up his thought.

'It wasn't your fault. You got that freelance assignment. You'd worked so hard to make them give it to you and nobody else—'

'Jobs had been a bit thin on the ground,' he recalled. 'We'd gone through your mother's money and I had nothing to show for it. I felt so ashamed of that, I'd have done anything to earn money. I didn't like going abroad on that job, but you seemed fine when I left—'

'Nobody could have guessed it was going to happen,' she said quickly. 'I was actually feeling very well that day, and then suddenly—'

'Go on,' he said after a moment.

'No, it doesn't matter.'

Her refusal was like a door slammed in his face, hurting with unexpected force. 'Why won't you tell me?'

'You always said there was no point in brooding about things,' she explained without rancour. 'You said we'd talk about it later, when I was pregnant again and talking wouldn't hurt.'

He winced. 'That was just to suit my own convenience,' he said harshly. 'I couldn't bear to speak about it, so I made it impossible for you. It was an act of pure selfishness, didn't you know that?'

She rested her head against his shoulder. 'I can't really remember now.'

He moved his free hand upwards until it found her face, cupping her cheek. Then he leaned his head down against her hair.

'Kelly, I'm sorry for everything,' he said quietly.

'Don't be. You were right. Brooding's no use. It wastes time. You have to think of what lies ahead of you.'

'Do you know what does lie ahead of you?'

'No. Not for a while yet. Maybe next week. If I'm still pregnant by next Tuesday—'

'Hush!' he stopped her quickly. 'You will be. I know that. I know it with total certainty. I promise you have nothing to worry about.'

She thumped him weakly on the shoulder. 'You so-and-so,' she said. 'You don't know what you're saying. You've no idea about babies or pregnancy, and you talk as though you're handing the word down from the mountain. So why do I believe you? Why can you make me believe you when I know you're talking through your hat?'

'Talking through my hat is what I'm good at,' he said wryly. 'My one and only skill. I've built a career on it, and I thought maybe I could put it to good use for a change. But I never fooled you. Still, it can be true, even if it's only me saying it. You're going to have this baby safely,' he repeated insistently, trying to convince her, not just with his voice but with the comforting warmth of his arms. 'And you can do the things you meant to the first time. You'll have it all back, everything you lost then.'

At once he knew he'd made a false step. Kelly tensed and drew away from him.

'What is it?' he asked anxiously.

'You don't understand. I can't have back what I lost then. That child is gone for ever.'

'But you'll have this child—'

'A different one. Not a replacement for the other. She'll always be my first child, my daughter, as long as I live.'

'Ah yes, I remember. You said it would have been a girl.'

'It *was* a girl,' Kelly insisted. 'Not would have been, was. She was a real person to me, even though she didn't quite make four months. She was real, and she died before I even knew her. All the time I was miscarrying I tried to talk to her, to tell her to hang on because her mother loved her. But then it was too late, so I said goodbye and told her that I always had loved her, and always would. But I don't know if she heard me.' Kelly's voice was suddenly thick with tears.

'Of course she did,' Jake said fiercely. 'Not heard, but felt what you were saying, sensed it. She *knew.* You have to believe that.'

'I try. Thank you for telling me that.'

I should have told you then, he thought, *but I didn't know any of this.*

He longed to ask if she'd told their child that he too loved her, but he no longer had any right. And he was afraid that Kelly, in her uncompromising honesty, would give him an answer he couldn't bear.

'And if the worst comes to the worst,' he added hesitantly, 'you're not alone. You've still got—your brother.' His arms tightened about her.

'Yes,' she murmured comfortably. 'I always wanted a brother. Maybe it was because I didn't have a father, but I used to dream of someone I could talk to, and who'd be strong for me, and perhaps need me too. I

was just a burden to my mother, and I thought how
nice it would be to have a brother who'd rely on me
as much as I relied on him.' She tightened her arms
about Jake. 'Who'd have thought it would turn out to
be you?'

'I don't know that I'm any better as a brother than
I was as a husband,' he said sombrely.

'You came looking for me tonight. You're solid and
you're here.'

'Which is more than I was—'

'Hush,' she stopped him. 'We've covered all that,
and it doesn't matter any more.'

'No,' he said quietly, 'I suppose it doesn't.' He bent
his head to kiss the top of her hair. 'Kelly,' he murmured, 'Kelly, Kelly... I'm so sorry.'

She looked up at him. 'No need to be sorry, Jake.
You made me very happy, lots of times.'

'But not all the time.'

'There isn't really any such thing as all the time,'
she said wisely. 'We shouldn't ask for it.'

'No, I guess not,' he sighed. 'But it was good now
and then, wasn't it?'

'Oh, yes, *yes*, the best thing in the world.' A radiant
smile broke over her face and Jake drew in his breath.

Very gently he laid his lips against her forehead,
kissing her like the brother he was supposed to be, and
they clung together contentedly until a shout startled
them.

'Oi!' They looked up to find a uniformed man standing a few feet away. 'I'm closing up now,' he called.
'You two go and do your courting somewhere else.'

Jake could have cheerfully strangled the man for ru-
ining the precious moment, but Kelly gave a choke of
laughter.

'We're going,' Jake called hastily, helping her to her feet. Then his sense of humour returned. 'Courting! If we told him the truth he wouldn't believe it.'

'Nobody would believe it,' she agreed. 'You have to be mad to understand.'

'And we always were.'

As they strolled away the lights began to go off. 'It was nice being mad together,' he mused.

'Mmm. It was lovely.'

'Come on.' He tried to hurry her. 'It's too cold out here for you.'

'You too. I'm supposed to be looking after you, remember?'

'Guess we'll have to look after each other.'

'For a while.'

'Yes—for a while.'

Kelly had said 'next Tuesday' and in her mind that was always the cut-off date. If she could hold out five more days, then four, then three, two…

On Monday night she worked late, reading first one book then another. The print passed under her eyes without her taking anything in. She knew what she was doing, making an excuse not to go to bed, because if she had to lie looking into the darkness the terrors would get worse.

There was a thin line of light under Jake's door, and she found herself looking at it with resentment. If he was up, why didn't he come and talk to her? That was what brothers were for, wasn't it?

Then her resentment died. This was the way she'd chosen it, with Jake kept at arm's length. She hadn't even told him the crucial fact that she was due to have an ultrasound scan the next day. She'd meant to, but

somehow there had always seemed a good reason for
not bothering him.

She sighed, telling herself to stop playing games and
face the truth. It was her pride that held her silent. He
might have thought she was asking him to involve himself more deeply in the pregnancy, and what she
dreaded most was to see him being determinedly polite
to cover his reluctance.

She took a deep breath, telling herself firmly not to
give in to weakness. She put the books tidily away and
went to her room, with a last hopeful glance at Jake's
door. The strip of light was still there, but nothing was
moving. She closed her own bedroom door very quietly.

Even so, Jake heard the faint sound. He'd detected
every movement she made and knew when she riffled
through books or paced the floor. He'd left his light on
deliberately, so that she would know he was up. At any
moment, he was sure she would knock and say she
needed him. Perhaps she would even tell him about the
scan she was having tomorrow, about which he would
never have known if he hadn't found the letter by
chance. It would happen. All he had to do was wait.

But he waited and waited, until at last he knew that
waiting was useless. He heard her bedroom door close,
and then there was nothing to do but put out the light.

At the hospital next day Kelly went to Maternity and
presented her card. While the receptionist tapped the
computer she looked around the waiting room, and
stared, with growing happiness, at what she saw.

'Jake? What are you doing here?'

He came forward from where he'd been hanging

back in the crowd. He looked awkward and self-conscious.

'Thought I'd hold your hand,' he said gruffly. 'I'll go away if you don't want me.'

Only now did she know how very much she had wanted him. And he had sensed it, and come here to be with her. A surge of emotion welled up in her without warning and she had to fight back tears.

'Kelly, are you all right?' He put his hands on her shoulders, looking alarmed.

'I'm fine,' she said huskily, annoyed with herself for nearly losing control. 'I'm pregnant. I'm allowed to have idiotic moods.'

'I don't think they're idiotic. What do you want me to do?'

'Stay. Please stay.' She slipped her hand into his as though to keep him there. As he guided her to a seat she said, 'But how did you know?'

'I found the letter lying around. I didn't mean to pry but—well, I suppose I did. I'm sorry. But you might have told me.'

'Yes, I should have done. Why were you hiding in the background?'

'I thought Carl might be with you.'

'No, he just dropped me off at the end of the road. He had a meeting to get to, something to do with his Easter dig.'

'What's that?'

'He's off studying ruins in Italy over the Easter vacation.'

'I think someone's trying to attract your attention,' Jake said, seeing a nurse waving.

She ushered them into a small room with a bed and a scanning machine.

'Ms Harmon?' she said. 'And this is—?'

'My brother,' Kelly said quickly.

'Right, Mr Harmon, if you'd like to sit here.'

'I'm not—' he started to say, then bit his lip and fell silent.

'If you'd lie down there…' The nurse indicated the couch.

Kelly hesitated for a moment, her eyes fixed on the couch. Jake understood. It was a strange sensation because he'd never understood before. He'd loved Kelly and been good to her within the limits of his nature, but the workings of her heart and mind had always been shrouded by a curtain of mystery. When she'd tried to tell him he'd grown tense because he often couldn't follow what she was saying. And she'd known, and stopped trying.

Now everything had changed. After the battering his body and his nerves had taken recently he seemed to have become alive to all the world, but mostly to her. The curtain had dissolved, leaving her inner truth revealed to him. This scan would finally answer all questions, and however much she tried to convince herself that the news was good and she only needed confirmation, at heart she was terrified.

So was he. For if things went wrong again her heart would break unbearably. And she would need him, and he would fail her. Because hadn't he always failed her?

'Come on,' he said, slipping a gentle arm around her.

She threw him a grateful smile and went to lay down on the couch, pushing her jeans down to her hips. The nurse spread a cool jelly over her bare stomach and took up a white gadget like a small box, attached to the machine. As she moved this back and forth over Kelly's stomach a picture began to form on the screen.

At first it was nothing more than a collection of shadows in different shades of grey, some light, some dark. When the nurse said, 'There's the head,' Jake stared, unable to make out any particular shape. He glanced at Kelly, but she was staring at the screen, transfixed, her face radiant. It seemed to Jake that she'd forgotten him. Then he felt a slight touch on his hand, and gradually Kelly's fingers intertwined with his. Still not looking at him, she gripped him, tightening the pressure until he was wincing. But nothing would have made him pull away.

'Can you see the head?' he murmured.

'Of course. There.'

And suddenly he could see it. What had been all confusion before settled into a head, a form, limbs.

'I can see hands and feet,' he breathed.

'And there's a good strong heartbeat,' the nurse confirmed. 'I believe your last pregnancy ended in miscarriage, Ms Harmon?'

'That's right. But I'm sure this one has lasted longer now.'

'Well, I can tell you, you've got a strong healthy child there. See where you can see thumping? That's the heartbeat.'

They both looked in awed silence while the little dot thumped softly away, with its message of life and hope. The nurse spoke but neither of them heard her. She spoke again, louder.

'I beg your pardon?' Kelly said, startled.

'I asked if you want to know the sex?'

'No, thank you,' she said, at exactly the same moment that Jake said, 'Yes.'

'All right,' Kelly said. 'Is it a boy or a girl?'

'No, do it your way,' Jake hurried to say. 'After all, it's not my decision. It doesn't really concern me.'

In his haste to do what she wanted he felt he might have put that better, but it was too late now.

'Very well,' Kelly said quietly. 'What is it?'

'A boy.'

She tried to see Jake's face. She thought she saw a brief expression of sadness, but he was looking steadily at the screen, and it was hard for her to be sure.

'He's moving around all the time,' he said in wonder. 'Punching and kicking. Does it hurt?' he added anxiously.

'I can't feel a thing,' she said, looking down at her stomach as though expecting to see it move. There was nothing to see, but the little creature on the screen was never still. Already it had its own world, its own life, separate from the turmoil going on outside.

The nurse gave them a picture from the screen. Jake took charge of it while Kelly adjusted her clothes. Once she glanced up, expecting to see him gazing at the little snap, but he never glanced at it, merely put it in his breast pocket, which he buttoned firmly.

Neither spoke as they left the hospital. As they descended the steps he drew her hand through his arm, to steady her, but they were both moving in a dream. At the foot of the steps he said, 'Come with me,' and drew her along the pavement towards the entrance to a shopping precinct.

Still without coming back down to earth, she asked, 'Where are we going?'

'To celebrate.'

'But this is a wool shop.' He was whisking her through the door.

'What better place to celebrate a baby? Good morning.' He advanced on the assistant. 'I want a ton of white wool—oh, and some blue—and every baby pattern you have.'

This was Jake in an exhilarated mood. There was no holding him back. He went through a sheaf of patterns, tossing each one aside as unsatisfactory.

'I like those bootees,' Kelly objected.

'Nah, these are better.'

'All right, we'll have these,' she said, grabbing a pattern as it flew past. 'And these rompers, and the bonnet.'

'How about—?'

'How much time do you think I have for knitting?'

He considered. 'I suppose I could do some? After all,' he added provocatively, 'if you can do it, how hard can it be?'

Laughing, she slapped him lightly on the arm, and was horrified when he made a sharp noise, visibly wincing. 'What did I do?' she asked, shocked.

'Nothing, I'm just a seven stone weakling.' He was laughing again, slightly pale, but he was always pale these days. 'We'll have these patterns, and this wool.'

They sailed out of the shop laden with wool which Jake insisted on carrying. He'd recovered from whatever had troubled him, and his step was jaunty. Kelly found her mood soaring to meet his. The first stunned realisation was giving way to joy. She gave a hop, and would have stumbled, but Jake saved her.

'Steady,' he said. 'You're going to have a baby.'

'Have you only just noticed?'

'It's only just become really true.'

'Yes, of course it has. I'm going to have a baby. Jake, *I'm going to have a baby!*'

She threw her arms about him, and he dropped the

wool to put his about her, hugging her tightly, while careful of the bump that was just beginning to show.

'It's all right,' he said urgently. 'Last time you lost it before this, but now you've got a healthy baby. *You're going to have a baby.*'

'I am, aren't I? I really am.'

'You really are.'

'Yes, I am,' she said, hearing herself becoming idiotic and not caring a bit.

'Yes, you are.' He was grinning, catching her mood.

The two of them began to giggle at the same moment, clutching each other, almost hysterical with relief and happiness. Passers-by regarded them with alarm and scuttled past while they shouted with laughter. Kelly clung to him tightly, her head pressed against his chest so that she could hear the soft thud of his heart deep within. And that made her think of the other beating heart, the one they'd seen together: their son.

CHAPTER NINE

THE weeks that followed were among the happiest Kelly had ever known. College had finished for the Easter vacation and she could stay at home all day, reading and making baby clothes, with Jake for company.

He'd never carried out his threat to start knitting, wisely deciding to leave it to the expert. Instead he bought a soft golden teddy bear that Kelly said was big enough to overwhelm any baby.

This was the pregnancy she'd dreamed of last time, with her child's father there, attentive, striving to be aware of her needs. The only thing that spoilt it was that he didn't know that he was the father.

Sometimes she wondered why she didn't tell him that the baby was his. He must surely suspect it, and might only be waiting for her confirmation.

But he never asked, and she wondered if he cared about the answer. He went out of his way to be the perfect brother, helpful and supportive, but it was as though he was responding at arm's length. However hard she tried, she could detect no sign that he wanted any other relationship than brother.

Until she knew more about what was happening inside his head she couldn't risk imposing what might be an unwanted burden on a man who was already coping with so much.

For his recovery still had some way to go. He didn't gain weight fast enough and his pallor didn't improve, and his strength would fade without warning. But his manner was cheerful and he always insisted that he felt fine. Once she mentioned consulting the doctor and he said firmly, 'Stop fussing,' in a way that reminded her of the old Jake.

She came home from shopping one day to find supper ready, but a supper such as she'd never seen before.

'Sardines and cornflakes?' she said, wide-eyed.

'You couldn't get enough of them last time.'

'But not together. Anyway, it's bananas this time.'

'You're craving bananas?' he echoed, disgusted. 'That's very unimaginative.'

'Boring, isn't it? In fact, I'm even more boring than that. It was a very mild craving and it's almost over.'

He looked injured. 'I was only trying to help.'

'I know you were, and I do appreciate it.'

'I just didn't get it right.'

'Well, if you really want to help me—'

'Anything, anything.'

'Don't say that so readily. You don't know what I'm going to ask.'

'It doesn't matter what it is. You have my absolute, binding, unbreakable promise.'

'Fine. Come to birth classes with me.'

'You tricked that promise out of me.'

'Oh, yeah! I never asked you for "absolute, binding and unbreakable."'

'Then let me off.'

'No way!'

'*Kelly—*'

She made a noise like a chicken clucking, and he glared. *'All right!'*

He kept his word, although with much protest, and arrived at their first class in a furtive manner that made her chuckle. But when he looked around and saw other, similarly uneasy characters hiding behind their pregnant woman, he seemed to relax. After that his journalist's mind took over, and by the time they left he'd taken in everything, and was able to discuss it sensibly as they went home.

'I knew I'd find it easy,' he said as they opened the front door. 'I can't think why you didn't want me to go.'

'Get inside and put the kettle on before I thump you,' she said sternly.

He grinned and scuttled inside, rubbing his hands with wicked glee. She smiled after him tenderly. Jake was wonderful when he was like this.

To prove it he made her put her feet up and brought her a bowl of bananas in milk. 'Peace offering.'

'Thanks. Yummy! This is just what I need before I go to bed. Nice and light, doesn't weigh heavily on the stomach. Glad you learned something from that class. I thought the whole thing was going over your head.'

'Yeah, sure!' he jeered, grinning.

She finished the bananas and leaned back, stretching out while he massaged her feet. 'That's good, that's good,' she sighed. 'Keep doing it.'

'Yes, dear.'

'Gotcha,' she shouted triumphantly.

'What?' He rubbed his ear.

'You used to swear that the one thing you'd never say was "Yes, dear."'

'I never.'

'You did, when we were first going out. You had this uncle who was henpecked. According to you, all he ever said to his wife was, "Yes, dear," and, "No, dear." You said you'd starve in the streets before saying it. In fact, you said it was the perfect reason for never marrying.'

And she'd cried herself to sleep that night.

'When did I say that?'

'About a month before we got married.'

'Well, that shows you. And if you're suggesting that I married you under duress, you're wrong. Now go to bed. You need your rest.'

He was right, but sometimes these days she found it hard to get to sleep. Now the sickness stage of pregnancy had passed and she was brimming with health and vigour. She understood just how much one morning when she surprised Jake coming out of the bathroom wearing only a towel around his middle.

He was too thin, and his glowing tan had gone, but it was still the body she remembered, and that excited her. Without warning she was swept by a physical desire so intense that it took her breath away. If she had imagined that pregnancy would save her from such feelings she knew now that she was wrong.

It was as though time had turned back to the night of the party, that hot, velvet night when she and Jake had cast aside restraint, becoming two vibrant, healthy animals, intent on pleasure. And he knew how to give a woman pleasure. The memories were still there in her flesh, sensitising her, so that the mere sight of him made her ache with need.

When he noticed her looking at him his eyebrows went up in a quizzical question, and she was suddenly conscious of the gap between her desire and the way she looked. How could he possibly respond by wanting this thickening figure? She mumbled something and got out fast. But that night she didn't sleep. Nor the next night.

She found that she could pace the floor for just so long. Then she had to think of something else, equally useless. She tried making sandwiches. She tried reading. Nothing worked because every time she closed her eyes he was there, touching her face, kissing her softly as a preliminary to making love. And when she opened her eyes again she was alone and desolate.

'Are you all right?' he asked one night, finding her in the living room, sipping tea. 'It's three in the morning. What are you doing up?'

'Just wanted a drink.'

'But you do this every night.' His voice changed, became gentle. 'What's the matter?'

'Nothing,' she said firmly.

Only that I'm going out of my mind with wanting you, she thought, *and getting less attractive by the day.*

'Come on, tell your brother.'

She almost laughed aloud. *This is one thing I can't tell my brother.*

When she didn't reply he changed tack and began to tell her funny stories. They were about nothing in particular, anecdotes from his colourful career with the intensity stripped out and only the humour left in. For the first time he admitted what she'd always suspected, that he hated flying.

'Sometimes I wonder how I landed up in a job where I fly all the time.'

'And of course Jake Lindley can't tell anyone,' she said gently.

'Jake Lindley laughs at danger. If he let on that his stomach was five miles behind nobody would ever take him seriously again.'

'And being taken seriously mattered to you, didn't it?'

'A lot. I wanted—hell, I can't remember what I wanted. It all seems so far away now. Doesn't the past seem that way to you?'

'Yes,' she said at once. 'Everything is shifting, and I've no idea where it's going to end up.'

He looked at her wryly, 'You still don't want to tell me what's on your mind, do you?'

'I can't. Honestly I can't.'

'Would you tell Carl?'

'No.'

'Then I guess it must be serious if you can't even tell Carl. Who could you tell?'

'Nobody.'

'Nobody. I guess that's the story of your life, isn't it? Nobody around to listen to what you want to say. You never really had anyone, not a father, not a real mother—'

'She did her best.'

'Then it was a rotten best. Why wasn't she around more to protect you from me? Any mother could have seen that I was a bad lot, and you were eighteen. She made it easy for me.'

'Be fair. She never tried to pressure me into giving the baby up. She let me marry you.'

'She was thrilled to see you marry me. It left her free. But it wasn't exactly the wedding a young girl dreams of, was it?'

'You don't know what I dreamed about,' she said lightly.

'Maybe I wasn't totally the blind clod I sometimes seemed. I remember we went to the wedding of one of your friends. It was in church, she had a white dress, bridesmaids, all the extras. I watched you. You were loving it. You'd have liked the same, wouldn't you?'

'Well—'

'But what you got,' he said, steamrollering over her, 'was a hurried little ceremony in a backstreet register office, wearing an ordinary day dress. And you never complained.'

'I didn't want to. I'd have liked to be married in church, but I didn't care about the trimmings.'

'You wanted a career, and you didn't get it,' he went on. 'You wanted a baby and didn't get one.'

'But—'

'Kelly tell me this—has anyone, in your entire life, taken care of you? I mean *really* taken care of you, put themselves out for you, cherished you, set your needs above their own?'

'But of course. You—'

'Come on!' he almost shouted. 'You know better than that. I put myself first, from start to finish.'

'I don't believe that.'

'Well, you should. You know as well as I do that I never—'

'Jake, stop it,' she said urgently. 'This can't do any good now.'

'I thought you'd want to hear that I share your low opinion of me.'

'Maybe I did once, but that's all over. We have a good arrangement here, but we mustn't spoil it by raking over the past.'

He shrugged. 'As you say. Let it go. What difference can it make now?'

She rose from her chair. The movement brought her slight swelling into focus, and he took her hands to help her the rest of the way.

'There's one thing you wanted that you're going to have,' he said. 'I'm glad about the baby, Kelly. Glad for your sake. That's something I don't want to spoil for you, and I promise that I won't.'

'Thank you,' she said in a strained voice. 'Goodnight, Jake.'

She had to get away from him before he suspected that she was on the edge of tears. If she hadn't stopped him he would have destroyed all her memories of their marriage. Bit by bit he would have gone through it, putting his own behaviour in the worst, unloving light. She'd always known that he didn't love her as she loved him, that he had married her to secure their child. But still she'd cherished the belief that he'd loved her a little. Without that belief the last eight years would be reduced to rubble. For a moment she almost hated him for trying to do that.

She was doing what she'd warned against: raking over the past. She'd taught herself to be stronger than that now. She took a deep breath, pulled herself together, and got into bed.

Jake also went to bed, moving slowly, partly to counter the dull ache in his insides that troubled him these days, but mostly with the crushing effects of disappointment.

Hell, what had he expected? That she would fall into his arms just because he owned past mistakes? She didn't need him to admit he'd been a lousy, selfish jerk of a husband. She already knew that.

But somehow he'd persuaded himself that her kindness might be more than kindness, which just showed what a fool he was. She hadn't even let him finish. His 'dear sister' was clinging to him for support because that was what she needed. And he, who'd sworn to give her whatever she needed, would have to be satisfied with that.

But still, he felt as though she'd slammed a door in his face.

It was good to see Carl's bronzed face on the first day back at college. In fact it was good to see everyone. Jake had ruined the morning by being in a foul temper from the moment he awoke. Nothing she'd said had been right. Everything she'd done had provoked his criticism, until he'd finally said, 'Don't be late home,' and she had grown cross.

'I'll come home when I'm ready. Stop smothering me, Jake.'

'Just trying to take care of you,' he'd snapped.

'Well, I feel as if you want to tie me down. Do this, don't do that, get home when I say.'

'All right, all right!' He'd thrown up his hands as if to fend her off. Later she was to remember that gesture with torment.

'I'll leave you alone then,' he'd growled, and slouched back to his room.

To her dismay she found it was a relief to get away from him to the safety of college, where she felt at home. Carl waved from a distance and mouthed 'See ya!' before vanishing into the crowd. She spent the day catching up with friends, checking timetables and getting lists of books to read. At the end of the day there was a reunion in the pub at which she became very jolly on orange juice. Just when she'd given up hope of seeing Carl, he appeared.

'Come and have a pizza with me before you go,' he said.

'Lovely. I'll just let Jake know.'

But when she called she got the answer-machine. She left Jake a message, saying she'd be late.

'He's probably slipped out to get a Chinese meal from the place on the corner,' she told Carl. 'Let's go.'

Over pizza he described his Italian trip. He was a good talker and his descriptions made her feel that doors and windows were opening for her. In this way the time slipped by without her noticing, until she looked at her watch and realised that she'd been there for three hours.

'Jake will wonder if I've been abducted by aliens,' she said, taking out her phone and hastily dialling.

But again she got the answer-machine.

'That's strange,' she mused. 'He can't have been out all this time.'

'Why not? He was well enough to go out that night I came over. He must be even better now.'

'Actually he's not. In fact he seems a little peaky—' She stopped and a horrible fear rushed over her. 'Carl, I've got to get home quickly.'

He didn't argue, but hurried out with her and sped her home in his car. As she got out she looked up to her own windows and saw a faint light, which increased her apprehension.

'Kelly, there's nothing to worry about,' Carl urged as they went up in the lift. 'He came home from wherever he was and forgot to switch the answer-machine off before he went to bed.'

'Yes, of course,' she said eagerly, but she still ran out of the lift to her front door.

The flat was very quiet. There was no sign of Jake, but there was a light under his door. Quietly she pushed it open, and was briefly reassured by the sight of him lying in bed. She went to him and touched him on the shoulder, making him turn to face her. What she saw made her hurry out to Carl.

'Call an ambulance, fast,' she said tersely, and ran back at once.

Jake's face was a horrible greyish colour, much as when she'd first seen him in hospital. His eyes glittered as if with pain, and he stared at Kelly as though wondering who she was.

'Jake, *Jake*,' she wept. 'Oh, God, why didn't I get home sooner?'

She took his hand. It was dry and hot.

'Kelly?' he whispered.

'What happened to you?'

His lips moved painfully. 'I'm all right. Did you have a good day at college?'

'Damn college!' she said violently. 'And damn you for not telling me you were ill! You weren't well this morning, were you?'

'Bit grim,' he admitted in a harsh whisper. 'Your first day back—didn't want to spoil—'

'Shut up!' she said. 'Shut up, shut up! How could you have been so stupid?'

'Just comes naturally, I guess.'

She was torn by self-condemnation. If he'd been stupid, so had she, to be fooled by the mask he presented.

'How long have you been bad?' she demanded fiercely.

'A few niggles for the past few weeks.'

'But why didn't you say?'

'We were having such a great time—I looked forward to your vacation—just us—no college. Didn't want to miss it.'

'I should have seen it this morning,' she said bitterly. 'But I was so full of myself—'

'But that's right,' he said, grasping her wrist with a

hand that felt alarmingly hot. 'You ought to be full of yourself. It's your turn. That's what we said.'

'I don't care what we said any more,' she told him passionately. 'Do you think any of that matters? Jake, I lov—'

'Kelly,' Carl's voice came urgently from the door. 'They're here.'

And suddenly the paramedics were in the room, taking over, lifting Jake onto a stretcher, hurrying him away to the waiting ambulance. And the dangerous moment was past.

She went with him to the hospital, not daring to speculate on what might have happened. She caught a brief glimpse of Dr Ainsley, but he was gone in a moment, hurrying to Jake's side. Carl, who'd followed the ambulance, had joined her by the time Dr Ainsley returned, smiling and reassuring.

'He's got a massive infection. That's not good, but it'll be OK now I've pumped some antibiotics into him. What puzzles me is that he must have been feeling grim for a while and said nothing. He should have been back in here before this.'

'Did you ask him why?'

'Yes, but he only muttered something about Easter that I didn't understand. He's too fever-ridden just now to make sense. Maybe he'll tell you later.'

'Can I see him?'

'Just for a minute.'

She went quietly into Jake's room. He seemed to be asleep, so she sat beside him. Only now could she relax enough to consider Jake's astonishing words.

We were having such a great time—just us.

If he'd admitted his illness earlier he'd have spent

her Easter vacation in the hospital, and they would have missed the sweet friendship of the last few weeks.

Jake stirred and opened his eyes. 'Hi,' he murmured.

'Are you feeling any better?' she asked tenderly.

'A lot. Do you want to go on being mad at me?'

'No, we'll take that as read. I'm sorry about this morning—yesterday morning now, I suppose. I shouldn't have snapped at you. You were rotten to me because you were feeling bad. You should have said something.'

'Yeah, like burden you on your first day back.'

'So when were you going to say something?'

'I thought I'd call the hospital when you'd gone, but I went to sleep. After that I couldn't find the energy. I put the answer-machine on and went to bed. When I awoke I got your message—'

'And you were waiting for me all that time? If only I'd known!'

'I didn't want you to know. By the way, did I see Carl in the flat, or was I hallucinating?'

'No, he was there. We went for a pizza and he drove me home.'

'Good for him. Is he waiting for you?'

'Yes.'

'Fine, then he can take you home.'

'All right.' She rose, meaning to lean over and kiss his forehead, but he'd already closed his eyes and turned away.

Carl was waiting. On the way home she explained everything.

'He's been sick for weeks and kept it quiet?' he exclaimed. 'Why would he be so dumb?'

'He's not dumb,' she said fiercely. 'He just wanted

to be with me during the vacation. I think that's great of him.'

'So do I, dumb but great.'

After that he wisely fell silent.

She didn't sleep that night. She was tortured by the memory of Jake's face as he saw her off, saying, 'Don't be late home.' It had been a plea. Why hadn't she understood that? Instead she'd flown at him, and he'd thrown up his hands in a kind of self-defence, too ill to fight her further.

I was supposed to be taking care of him, she thought wretchedly. *A fine nurse I make!*

She barely concentrated at college next day, and left at the first moment, clutching books and heading for the hospital. Her head was full of things she needed to say to Jake.

He was a good colour, and she could see the antibiotics were taking effect.

'Sure I'm better,' he said in answer to her question. 'You know me—bounce back from anything.'

'You might not have bounced back from this. Dr Ainsley said things were getting serious.'

'OK, OK, I got macho, wouldn't admit I was sick, and now I'm paying the price. I'm sorry if I was a nuisance.'

'You weren't a nuisance. I really enjoyed the last few weeks, and I was glad to have you there—'

'We aim to please. I'm getting quite good at breathing exercises.'

Something determinedly bright in his voice made her look at him closely, and she saw what she dreaded. He was wearing his good humour like a mask. It kept her out.

Before she left Dr Ainsley told her, 'The infection stopped him digesting properly, that's why he's stayed so thin. I'll keep him here a couple of weeks, and when he goes home he should make giant strides. How are you managing? Is he a trial—apart from this, I mean?'

'No, it's been lovely,' Kelly said. 'Especially these last few weeks.'

'When he goes home it'll be better still.'

But she doubted that. Those few weeks alone together had been a wonderful time, but they were over.

She knew she'd been right when Jake left the hospital looking fitter than at any time since he was wounded. In the early days of his convalescence the hours and days had passed slowly, but now she found the time beginning to speed past. At last she could see that Jake's strength was coming back. He gained weight, his voice grew stronger, he was more like the old Jake Lindley.

He seemed conscious of it too, for there were no more of the intimate chats she'd come to rely on. His attention was turning outwards again, and she knew that was a good sign. He was friendly, kind and co-operative, but their past history might not have existed.

Any day now he would be ready to leave her and return to the life of success, glitter and Olympia. When that time came she would accept it without bitterness, thankful for what they had enjoyed, which had been so much better than she had dared to hope.

CHAPTER TEN

WITH every day Kelly found her new self becoming more settled, more truly *her*. There was no going back to that uncertain girl who'd waited on Jake's decisions. This mature woman made her own decisions, and if they hurt that was all the more reason for carrying them out decisively.

So as she saw Jake recovering, reaching the point where he would inevitably leave her, she decided to make the first move. Pride demanded it, and pride would soon be all she had to sustain her.

One day she said, 'Isn't it time you made a serious effort with Olympia?'

'What exactly do you mean by that?'

'Oh, come on, Jake. She's one of the "movers and shakers", isn't she? You always said they were the people who counted. It's time you were moving and shaking with her.'

He regarded her curiously. 'Would you care to define moving and shaking?'

Her shrug was a masterpiece of light-hearted indifference. 'Whatever grabs you. Maybe it's time to let Olympia grab you. Your call.'

'Does that mean what I think it means?'

'It means anything you like. Just don't let the grass grow under your feet.'

Incensed, he glared at her. 'You think I'm the kind of guy who'd sleep with a woman to get a job?'

'I only meant keep on her good side.'

'You meant a heck of a sight more than that.'

'Jake, I don't care why you sleep with her—'

'Or *if* I sleep with her?' he asked dangerously.

She wanted to shout, *You stupid man, of course I care. I love you and when you go I'll feel that my life's over for a second time. Why can't you see that?*

But he couldn't see it, and that told her what she really wanted to know. Jake's blindness was a form of self-protection. So she would hold her head up, make it all easy for him, and do her weeping when he'd gone.

She said lightly, 'We covered that a long time ago. It's a dead subject. All I ask is that you don't do it here, while I'm trying to write an essay about the pyramids.'

'Well, I'll be damned! You're a cool one.'

Her very coolness had seemed to enrage him. In a burst of temper he called Olympia, speaking honeyed words of wine and candle-light. And before Kelly knew it they'd made a date for the next evening, and she was left reflecting that she had only herself to blame.

Since it was too late for regrets, even if she would have allowed herself anything so spineless, she became 'Anne of Cleves' with a vengeance, helping him get ready the following day.

'You want to make a good impression,' she protested when he complained. 'Not the red tie. It's awful.'

'You gave it to me.'

'Did I? I must have been annoyed with you. The other one's better.'

'Olympia gave me that one.'

'Good for her. She's got better taste than me. She'll be flattered if you wear it.' Kelly sniffed the air appreciatively. 'Nice aftershave. Did she give you that too?'

'No, I bought it today.'

'Well, it's terrific. It'll drive her wild.' She brushed his shoulders, stood back to admire him, and asked, 'Have you got everything?'

'Everything.'

'Money? Credit card?'

'Got them.'

'Second credit card in case the first one's over the limit and they cut it up—?'

'Kelly, for Pete's sake!'

'It happened to you once, and it was the only one you had and you were stranded—'

'Yes, I remember,' he said edgily. 'I had to call you.'

'Pen?'

'Pen.'

'Matching socks?'

'Matching socks.'

'Clean underwear?'

'*What?*'

'In case you have an accident and they take you to hospital,' she said innocently. 'That's what my mother always used to say.'

'Mine too. I could never persuade her that if I was injured my underwear would be the last thing on my mind.'

They shared a grin. 'Off you go,' she said. 'Have a wonderful time.'

'Thanks. I intend to.' He eyed her seven-month bulge. 'You OK?'

'Never better. You are going to be really late coming in, aren't you?' She managed to sound hopeful.

'I may be away all night.'

'Oh good,' she enthused.

There was a kind of triumph in fooling him so completely. But it was a bleak triumph, and when he'd

gone she sat down with her arms folded over her body
and rocked back and forth in grief.

The restaurant was the most expensive he could find.
The wine was the finest in their cellar, the food the
most exquisite *cordon bleu*. Jake had chosen the details
with great care because tonight he was finally going to
break free.

He didn't define to himself exactly what, or whom,
he was going to break free from. It couldn't be Kelly,
because she denied that any ties bound them together.
The nearest he could come was breaking free of the
shackles of the past, something Kelly herself had
clearly done. This would prove he'd moved on as much
as she had.

Kelly's behaviour had unnerved him. It was nothing
short of insulting that she should have tossed him into
Olympia's arms. There would be no going back from
tonight, and it seemed that was what she wanted.

But he'd kept his thoughts to himself as Kelly fussed
around him and shooed him out of the flat. To have
protested would have been a point to her in the ironic
game they seemed to be playing. And if there was one
thing he wouldn't do it was let this infuriating, unrea-
sonable woman know that she'd gone one up.

And now here he was, in a restaurant with Olympia,
knowing that somehow he had to pass the night in her
bed, because just who did Kelly think she was to goad
him like that?

'I always knew this would happen at last,' Olympia
said, smiling at him, two little candles reflected in her
eyes. She reached over and took his hand in hers, giving him a front row view of her glacial beauty. Jake
had to admit she was stunning. Her black silk dress

was low cut, revealing the swell of her breasts, magnificent and tempting. Her hair was arranged in soft, fluffy curls, that danced about her face whenever she laughed.

She'd looked that way once before, on the night in Paris, when he'd been able to think of nothing but seducing her. He remembered the fierce temptation. If she hadn't led him to her room when she had he might have seized her and possessed her right there on the floor.

And then, when her door had closed behind them, and the great moment had come—it had all died. Because Kelly had been there, waiting for them. In reality she'd been hundreds of miles away, but somehow there too, watching him with so much love in her eyes that his heart had failed him. But she wouldn't be around to spoil things for him tonight, and Jake watched the curls that danced around Olympia's face.

Olympia's fingers gently caressed his hand, promising magical things to come.

'There've been so many obstacles keeping us apart,' she murmured. 'But we were bound to overcome them. Didn't you feel that too?'

'I guess I did. I haven't had a clear head for a long time—'

'My dear, I do understand. It must have been such a terrible shock for you. And not being able to work must have driven you crazy.'

'That's true,' he reflected. 'Not my usual kind of work, anyway.' He gave a self-mocking grin. 'I'm becoming a dab hand with the vacuum cleaner.'

'I'm sure you're making the best of it, but the nightmare's nearly over.'

'What nightmare?'

'Being trapped in that place with the "little woman" fussing over you, never giving you any peace.'

'The little woman is usually too busy with her college work to fret about me,' he said wryly.

'That's what she lets you think, but you know what she's really after, don't you? She wants you back.'

'Not her. She never wanted me there in the first place.'

'Oh, darling, don't be fooled. It's all an act.'

'Well, it's a very funny act, then. She cares about college and her baby. I'm just there on sufferance.'

'That's what she lets you think, but the bottom line is that you're *there*, living with her, just as she wants.'

Jake looked at her curiously, wondering how one human being could so misread another. 'It's not like that at all,' he said. 'Kelly's left me behind. She's changed; she—' He stopped because Olympia had given a delicate little yawn. 'I'm sorry.'

'Darling Jake, I want to concentrate on you tonight, not Kelly. I'm sure she's a dear little soul, and of course I'm grateful to her for taking you in and being a good nurse, but it's *you* that's left *her* behind, whatever she likes to pretend. What do you think she'd do if she knew that you were with me now? She'd go wild with jealousy.'

This left Jake in something of a quandary, since a gentleman could hardly tell a lady that he was planning to sleep with her at the urging—practically the orders—of another lady. Man-like, he took refuge in cowardly silence.

'You're right, we shouldn't be talking about her,' he said hastily.

'What time is she expecting you in?'

'She—er—knows I'm going to be very late.'

'Well, it's probably very good for her to get rid of you for a night.'

'What do you mean by that?' Jake asked, more sharply than he'd intended.

'Have you thought what a strain it must be for her, looking after you when she's pregnant?'

'We look after each other,' Jake said firmly.

Olympia gave a tinkling little laugh. 'What a charming idea. But I'll bet she does most of the work. At least, I hope she does. She's probably stretched out on the bed right now, getting a much needed rest.'

She'll be stretched out on the bed, all right, Jake thought. *What I want to know is, where's Carl?*

He pulled himself together and seized the champagne bottle. 'Have a little more champagne, darling. You're looking glorious tonight.'

She gave him the serene, self-confident smile of a goddess accepting tribute, and squeezed his hand. Jake reminded himself that he'd been out of action for a long time, which was doubtless the reason for a mysterious sense of unease that was haunting him. He returned the pressure of her hand and looked deep into her eyes, thinking of the night to come. But inside him there was only a mysterious and terrifying blank—as blank as Olympia's eyes. How could a man look deep into eyes like that? There was nothing behind them.

He had a feeling of moving through a dream as they toasted each other in champagne and left the restaurant, finding a cab at once. As they sat in the back Jake tried to pull himself together. A man who'd made a decision should get on with it, without hassle. He took her into his arms and she melted against him, all fragrant femininity. How cold her lips were, he thought. He could feel his heart pounding and tried to believe that this was passion, but somehow it didn't feel right. The lights outside the cab seemed to be whirling past at a tremendous rate. He crushed Olympia to him, pressing his lips against hers in an attitude of urgency.

Olympia lived in an elegant apartment block in one of the more expensive parts of town. As they crossed the vestibule Jake felt soft carpet beneath his feet. The lift was grey and mirrored, with faint piped music overhead.

Her home was like the woman herself: exquisite, modern, with nothing out of place. As soon as the door had closed behind them she slid her arms about him again, murmuring urgently against his mouth.

He did what was expected of him, kissing her fiercely to blot out the absence of anything behind the kiss.

'Your heart's thumping,' she whispered. 'You really want me, I can tell.'

He made a throaty, inarticulate sound that she could interpret as she pleased. Whatever she thought, his body was dead and empty of desire. Cold sweat stood out on his brow at the thought of backing off a second time.

'Come with me,' she murmured against his mouth. 'I'm going to make this a really special occasion.'

She unzipped her dress and allowed it to fall to the ground. Jake fixed his eyes on her charms, hoping desperately that something would happen soon. But nothing did, even when she pulled off his jacket and began to work on the buttons of his shirt.

She took his hands and guided them to the fastening of her bra. His fingers worked mechanically until the clasp gave and her breasts were free, swelling heavily against his fingers in a way that should have inflamed him to madness. Instead, it was like touching plastic.

After this there would be no way back to Kelly—*no way back*—

Suddenly Jake felt himself falling. He clutched the wall and stared about him, wondering where he was, and what he was doing here with this woman.

'Jake?' Olympia's puzzled voice came from a great distance. 'Are you all right?'

He wasn't all right. Nothing would ever be all right again. The whole world was moving now, whirling, spinning him into a void. Everywhere was darkness, but nowhere was the darkness worse than in his mind. His surroundings, the woman he was with, what he'd been about to do, all seemed horribly futile.

Olympia was grasping his shoulders, staring into his face. 'Jake! Jake, what's the matter?'

He couldn't answer. He was shaking violently and now he knew that the pounding of his heart had nothing to do with desire. It was fear, horror. The sound increased until it filled the world, a deafening echo, full of the bleak tones of despair. This was more than the dread of a man trying to make love and discovering that he couldn't. He was lost in a howling wilderness from which Olympia had no power to rescue him.

He struggled to take deep, gasping breaths, but he was suffocating. It was like being pulled towards a black hole. An immense force was drawing him ever closer to the moment when he would be tossed into the hole for ever, sucked down into madness. He fought as best he could, but he seemed to have no strength left. It was pointless to fight when there was nothing but fear and misery in the whole universe.

'Jake, pull yourself together!'

Somehow Olympia's voice penetrated the fog about his consciousness. She was shaking him.

'What's the matter with you?' she demanded. 'Are you ill? Do you want a doctor?'

'No,' he managed to say. 'Not a doctor.'

He knew who he wanted, but it took all his strength to reach the telephone and dial the number of the one person in the world who could help him.

Dear God, let her be there! Please, please let her be there.

The phone on the other end began to ring.

She's always been there for me before. Make her there now.

The ringing went on and on.

She's not there. But she must be. She has to be because I need her. Please, please, please, please, please...

'Hello?' Kelly answered.

The relief was so great that he almost passed out. 'Kelly,' he said in a croak that sounded nothing like his usual voice.

'Who is this?'

'It's me—Jake—'

'Jake, whatever's the matter? Are you ill?'

'I don't know,' he gasped. 'I'm at Olympia's apartment—can you come here—please come—I want to get home and I can't—' He was heaving for breath again.

'Of course I'll come,' she said at once. 'But, Jake, can you tell me what's happened?'

'I don't know what's happened,' he whispered. 'But get here quickly.'

He dropped the phone and leaned back against the

wall, shaking in every limb. Olympia had followed the
conversation with outrage.

'Whatever's come over you?' she asked, taking him
by the shoulders and giving him a shake.

'I have to go home. Sorry, Olympia. I'm not—very
good company—tonight—'

'It's not your fault,' she said in a voice of concern.
'You tried to do too much too soon.'

'Right,' he muttered, hardly knowing what he said.

'You're still worse than we thought.'

'Right.' He would agree to anything if only Kelly
would arrive soon.

'I think you should go back to the hospital,' she said
firmly.

'Not—hospital—Kelly.' He gasped the words out,
one by one.

'Come and sit down.' She steered him to the sofa,
where he almost collapsed.

Olympia left him for a moment while she collected
her scattered clothes and vanished into her bedroom.
While there she made a phone call.

Jake stared at something on the floor, wondering
what it was and what he was supposed to do with it.
At last it registered as his shirt, which he must have
discarded some time before. He couldn't remember it.
Using all his concentration he lifted it and put it back
on. The effort exhausted him and he slumped on the
sofa, fixing his attention on the wall opposite. If he
watched the pattern hard enough he could avoid thinking about the monster that was fighting to break out of
its cage in his mind.

It was strange how perfectly regular the pattern
was—one, two, three—how long would it take her to
get here?—four, five, six—when had he phoned her?

He'd lost track of time—seven, eight, nine—but, please God, let her be here soon?

He reached the end of the row and started again. One, two, three—how would she come? In a cab?—four, five, six—it was such a distance—such a vast distance from Kelly to Olympia—an unbridgeable distance—why did he think of that now? Seven, eight, nine—

He kept his eyes closed, trying to shield his inner self from Olympia's curious gaze. There was only one person he trusted to see deeply into his heart and soul, but she wasn't here. She had promised to come to him, but where was she? The monster was growing stronger, smashing against the bars, threatening him with unspeakable horrors. If she didn't get here in time…

The doorbell broke into his terrors. His forehead was damp with relief. Now everything would be all right.

But it wasn't Kelly. It was two men in grey sweaters and trousers.

'Are you the lady who called the ambulance?' one of them asked Olympia.

'That's right.'

'What the devil have you done?' Jake demanded harshly. 'Who asked you to call anyone?'

'Darling, you need help.'

'And I'll get it when Kelly arrives.'

'I mean real professional help.'

Jake turned on the two men, gasping. 'Who are you and where do you come from?'

'Forest Glades,' one of them said. 'The best private rest home in the business.'

'Be damned to you and your "rest home". I know what that means.'

'It's all right,' Olympia soothed. 'The company will pay the bills.'

With a tremendous effort he pulled himself together. The next words came out sounding strange to his own ears, harsh and dead, like a robot. But they made a sort of sense.

'I'm going home with my wife. She'll be here in a moment.'

The two men looked at Olympia, who gave an awkward laugh.

'Darling, you don't have a wife. You're divorced.' An ominous concern shaded her voice. 'Surely you remember? Of course I know you've been a bit forgetful recently—'

'I haven't forgotten the important things,' he said, still in the same harsh voice. 'Divorce or no divorce, Kelly is still my wife, and she always will be.'

'Jake, really—'

'And if you want proof of that, she's having my baby.'

The paramedics looked at him, then at Olympia. Jake was alive to the nuances but he was beyond caring. Every fibre of his being was concentrated on seeming normal until Kelly arrived. He could feel his control slipping, but if he could just hang on a little longer…she could handle everything…she was strong…she had always been strong…

'Excuse me,' came a voice from the doorway. The paramedics had left it open and Kelly was standing there, smiling and apparently at ease.

'Jake, dear,' she said, coming forward to him, 'I got here as soon as I could. Are you ready to come home now?'

'Yes,' he said hoarsely.

'Excuse me, miss—ma'am—' it was one of the paramedics '—can you confirm that you're his wife?'

Eyes wide with apparent naivety, Kelly declared, 'Of course I am. But you already knew that. He told you.'

So she'd heard, Jake thought. Everything was reaching him from a distance, but he registered that Kelly was totally in control.

The other paramedic was a puritanical young man. Eyeing Kelly's very obvious pregnancy with outrage he said stiffly, 'I'm sorry to tell you, ma'am, but we found your husband with this—lady.'

Her disconcerting response was a ripple of laughter. 'Haven't you given up yet, Olympia? I suppose you thought your best chance was to pounce now, while I'm pregnant. It doesn't seem to have worked, does it? Never mind, better luck next time.'

'You mean you don't mind?' the young man asked, gaping.

'Mind about her? What for? She's no threat to my marriage. Sorry, Olympia, but the truth is the truth, even when it hurts.'

'I think you'd better leave,' Olympia said through clenched teeth.

'Glad to,' Kelly said promptly, slipping her hand through Jake's arm. 'I'm sorry you two gentlemen were called out for no reason. Ready, darling?'

'One moment before you go,' Olympia said acidly, vanishing into the bedroom. She returned a moment later and held out her hand, bearing Jake's cufflinks. 'Don't forget these.'

'Thank you,' Kelly said, taking them. She met her gaze. 'Poor Olympia,' she said softly.

The murderous look in the other woman's eyes provided one of the great moments of her life.

CHAPTER ELEVEN

AFTERWARDS Jake had very little memory of leaving Olympia's apartment, or of getting home. The ride down in the lift blended into the cab Kelly had left waiting outside the building, getting into the back, taking refuge in Kelly's arms. She held him close, rocking him gently, murmuring words of comfort to ease an agony that she didn't understand. When they reached the flat she thrust money at the driver, still holding Jake's hand in her own, and drew him quickly into the building. When they were safely home she enfolded him again in a passion of protectiveness.

'You're shivering,' she said.

'I can't stop,' he said through chattering teeth.

'I'll put the heating on.'

'No, it's not that kind of shivering.'

'Jake, can you tell me what happened?'

'I don't know,' he said hoarsely. 'I don't know. Suddenly everything was dark and there was nothing in the world but fear and despair. But then I remembered there was you, and I knew if I reached you I'd be safe. Hold me. *Hold me!*'

'Yes, darling, yes—' The word slipped out without her knowing. 'I'm here. Hold onto me.'

She too was in a kind of shock, stunned by the suddenness with which the world had turned on its head. She'd sent him off to Olympia, telling herself that she was doing the best thing for both of them. In her mind she'd followed every step of his evening: the romantic

153

candlelit dinner, the journey back to Olympia's apartment, the soft music as they undressed and went to bed.

She'd tried to shut her thoughts off at this stage but it had been impossible. She knew Jake's body as nobody else would ever know it. She knew how he made love, the little caresses that excited him. She'd known him both as a tender, considerate lover, and a fiercely thrilling one. Which would he be with Olympia?

And then, when her torment was at its height, he'd called her, imploring her help.

Now she sat beside him on the sofa, feeling his trembling abate, wondering what terrors had invaded him, and why suddenly at this moment? She didn't press him to talk; he wasn't ready. It was enough that he was in her arms, needing her as never before.

He had said she was his wife, as though their marriage was an unbroken continuum. And he had claimed her child as his, as though in his heart he had always guessed. But he had not said these things to her, only to others, and perhaps they'd been only the desperate words of a desperate man. She would know nothing until he repeated them to her.

She, in her turn, had called him her darling, and she knew that it had always been true. Her love had never died. She'd merely buried it, hoping to forget how to find it again. Now she knew that had been a vain hope. While Jake retained even a shadow of his old cocky self she could fence with him, bicker with him, defend herself from him. But his vulnerability broke her heart. As long as he needed her, she was his.

'You're cold,' she said at last. 'You should be in bed.'

He seemed unable to move, as though he was drained of will, but he let her urge him to his feet and into the bedroom. She was shocked at the sight of him. His face had the muddy pallor of an old man's and there were black smudges beneath his eyes.

'Stay with me,' he whispered. 'I don't want to be alone. *Please, Kelly.*'

'Of course I will, my dear. I'll do whatever you want. Just let me get my things.'

She slipped away. She was gone just a couple of minutes, but when she returned, dressed for bed, Jake was standing at his door, watching for her with something in his eyes that it hurt her to see.

'I'm coming,' she said quickly, taking his hand.

As they lay together in bed he told her about the evening, keeping back nothing.

'I was going to take her to bed,' he said bluntly, 'but I couldn't. There was nothing there for her. Nothing. Just like last time.'

'Last time?'

'In Paris. I always told you the truth about that. I backed off at the last minute. You seemed to be there, and you wouldn't let me do anything that would destroy our love. So I made excuses and got drunk. And then the joke was that you wouldn't believe me. But it was true all the time.'

'I believe you now,' she whispered. 'I wish I'd believed you then, but I didn't know you in those days as I do now.'

He fell silent and she just held him, knowing that he must take his own time. Inwardly she was weeping for him.

'It was like sliding down into the pit of hell,' he said at last. 'As though my mind has been holding all the bad things behind bars and now they've got out. I don't know what to do.' He tried to force himself to speak sensibly. 'Of course it's only temporary. I'm all right now.'

But his voice shook even as he said it, and she tightened her arms.

'It *will* be all right,' she promised. 'I'll call the doctor tomorrow—'

Some old reflex action made him bristle at the word. 'I don't need a doctor—'

'Yes, you do,' she said firmly. 'No argument. I've decided.'

At that he even managed a shaky laugh. 'Yes, dear.'

She picked up the echo, as he'd intended, and smiled into the darkness. But her heart was heavy because she knew they'd just embarked on the dreadful road that Dr Ainsley had warned her about. It was sharp and thorny, and the end of it was hidden from her.

When she called the doctor next morning she was half afraid Jake would protest again, but he was too deep in his own private agony to say anything.

The local doctor was a brisk, well-meaning man with little imagination. To him, clinical depression was something to be treated with drugs, and time would do the rest. The medication he prescribed was strong and usually effective. Kelly learned that much from a talk with a fellow student who was doing medical research. But she felt the doctor had looked at only one side of the problem. Jake needed more. From the way he'd reached out to her she guessed it was something only she could give, but as yet she wasn't certain what it was. She could only watch and wait, and hope that the moment would find her ready.

Jake had never before suffered clinical depression. He'd thought he had, when he was first in the hospital.

Now he knew that experience had been nothing, just a bout of being down in the dumps—bad enough, but not to be compared with this bleak hell.

The medication was only partly effective. It dulled the edge of his consciousness, so that instead of the darkness being full of sharp weapons to taunt him it was a place of diffuse misery.

By day he slumped into coma-like sleep, by night he lay awake tormented by demons. They came from inside him, and had names like futility, guilt, hopelessness. From this perspective his entire past life seemed empty, his future non-existent.

His body seemed to be made of lead so that dragging one foot in front of another was an almighty effort. He understood nothing that was happening to him. Faces came and went. Voices echoed in his head. There was Kelly telling him that all would soon be well because Dr Ainsley had predicted this.

'He thought it would happen sooner…and then you recovered…you were so strong, it was like you'd got away with it…'

You were so strong…

He tried to remember when he'd ever really been strong. What had his strength ever been but an illusion, depending on one crucial prop? Then the prop had been removed and he'd seen himself with awful clarity. While Kelly was there, Jack the lad, a bouncing firecracker who could enthral the world. Without her, nothing.

Day after day his misery blotted out almost everything else and the world reached him through a fog. The only reality was Kelly, who had quietly moved her things back into his room, and spent each night with him in the double bed. When the fog was heaviest her face was still there, tense with anxiety, watching him with fearful eyes. She took several days off, making various unconvincing excuses, and gradually it dawned on him that she was afraid to leave him alone.

That brought the darkness down again. Her chance was slipping away because of him. History was repeating itself, and it mustn't be allowed to happen.

'It's all right,' he told her, concentrating hard on the words. 'I'll still be here when you get back. I'm not—going anywhere.'

At last he persuaded her to leave, and endured several hellish hours when the walls seemed to be closing in on him. But when she returned at the end of the day he managed a smile.

'The kettle's on,' he said with a fair pretence of cheerfulness. 'Sit down while I make you some tea.'

'How have you been?' she asked, looking anxiously into his face.

'It's getting easier,' he lied.

He knew she doubted him, and he managed to keep smiling until he was in the kitchen. There his control slipped and he stood clinging onto a shelf, heaving with distress while sweat poured down his face. But a movement behind him made him pull himself together and hoist the bright mask into place before she saw his face again.

He had his reward next morning, when she left the apartment with an easier mind. He gave her a cheery wave through the window before turning away as the waves of blackness engulfed him again.

Once he called Dr Ainsley. 'Kelly said you knew this was going to happen.'

'You took two bullets, and that's enough to traumatise any man,' Ainsley said cheerfully. 'Inside, you never did recover quite as well as you made out, and pretending just makes things worse. What medication are you taking?' When he heard he grunted. 'That's all right. It's good stuff. Give it time to do its work and leave the rest to Kelly.'

As days passed the fog lifted a little but the world still reached him at a distance. He read his mail, only half taking it in, but stray words and phrases clung, worrying him. Somewhere out there were things he should be thinking about, taking seriously, but they were muffled, and what could he do about them anyway?

One night he managed to sleep for a few minutes, then awoke sharply. There was a light under the door. He forced himself up and went out, to find Kelly lying on the sofa, frowning as she read a book. Something about her struck him forcibly.

'You're going to have a baby,' he whispered.

She jumped up, full of alarm. 'Jake—'

'It's all right, I'm not crazy.' He let her draw him down until he was sitting beside her. 'I knew you were pregnant—I did, didn't I?'

'Yes,' she said gently, 'you knew.'

'I remember now.' He shook his head as though trying to free it of a swarm of bees. 'There's something I can't quite—why are you sitting here alone?'

'I'm fine—'

'Why does nobody ever protect you?' he asked wildly. 'Why is it always you doing the caring? Your husband should have protected you, but we all know about him, don't we?'

'I don't think anybody really knew about him,' Kelly said gently.

'A jerk. He let you down all the time. Now he's letting you down again.'

'What do you mean by that?'

'I'll show you.'

He hauled himself up and made his way back to the bedroom, returning with a paper which he put into her hand. It was a bank statement showing that his money was fast vanishing.

'Not just a jerk, but a stupid jerk,' Jake said morosely. 'He never bothered to save when times were good. He spent it all on enjoying life.'

'He spent it on his wife too,' Kelly remembered. 'All those presents—'

'Which weren't what she wanted. When trouble came he didn't have any savings. After I was shot the firm's insurance company made a pay-out, although they used a technicality to make it as little as possible. That's what we've been living on. I thought I'd be back at work long before now, because I was ''Jake Lindley'' who could cope with anything. But look at me. A mess.'

Kelly was staring at the bank statement and a resolution was forming in her head.

'Say something, please,' he begged.

'All right.' She put her hands on his shoulders and looked into his face. She was about to take a huge risk, and she called all her love to help her judge the size of the gamble.

Vaguely she knew that she'd misjudged once before, driving him into Olympia's arms, helping to bring this nightmare down on him. If she misread him again she might condemn him to disaster, but if her courage failed he might languish in his present misery forever.

'I'll say this,' she told him. 'I think it's about time you started work again.'

He stared. 'You think anyone's going to give me work as I am?'

'You're not going to wait for people to give you work. You can make your own. It's time you started on that book you always talked about. Heaven knows you've got the material. All your experiences in so many countries, and then getting shot. That book will sell, if you write it quickly. Leave it too long and the moment will pass. You've got all this time at home. Use it.'

In the silence she saw the dawning of interest in his eyes. 'Do you—really think I could?'

'I know you could. Jake Lindley can do anything.'

'No—no,' he shook his head in agitation. 'This isn't "Jake Lindley". I'm not sure he'll ever be around again. It's just Jake.'

She understood.

'It was always Jake for me,' she said. 'I never much cared for "Jake Lindley".'

'But a book—I haven't done a long project in ages—I work in soundbites now—'

'Then stop working in soundbites and start having long, joined-up, thought-out opinions again,' she said urgently. 'Jake, you still have all that. You haven't lost it, just mislaid it a little.'

She was gripping his hands, looking eagerly into his eyes, and at that moment she looked closer to the seventeen-year-old who'd first adored him than he'd seen for a long time. It was the haunting echo of that memory that made him say, 'I'll do it—if you think I can—even though my head's full of cotton wool, so that I can't think how to put two words together.'

'You don't have to write it yet. Just do a bit of research and work out the outline. You can sell that to a
publisher first.'

'You've got it all worked out, haven't you?' he said
with a touch of admiration. 'You'll be wanting com-
mission as my agent next.'

'You bet I will!'

He almost laughed, and for a moment she thought
she'd revived the spark in him, but then his face became drained again.

'Kelly, this is crazy. I can't embark on the long haul
when it's as much as I can do to struggle up out of the
pit every morning.'

'Forget the long haul,' she said firmly. 'You're looking at it the wrong way.'

'Am I?' He was watching her closely, as if waiting
for her to produce the key that would open the vital
door.

'Just think about the first step. When you've done
that we'll worry about the second step, but never more
than one at a time. So you must decide what the first
step actually is.'

She was looking at him, waiting for a decision, and
he fought to clear his mind, which had become cotton
wool again. The first step...the first step...

'My notes,' he said at last. 'I need to go back over
them—and tapes—things from the last few years—to
refresh my memory—'

'Good. Where are they?'

'In my flat. I'll have to go there—'

'First thing tomorrow.'

It was barely dawn when she called a cab and they
went to his flat together. But when they reached the
front door she hesitated.

'Would you rather I waited out here?'

'Why should I want that?' he said, puzzled.

'You wouldn't let me come here before, to fetch your clothes. You sent Olympia.'

'Olympia's never been here. A social worker attached to the hospital did it for me. I guess I just didn't want you to see it.'

She began to understand when he opened the door. This was no home, but a soulless cage. One room to live in, one to sleep in, and nothing that spoke of the man who lived there. It was as though his real self had gone somewhere else on the day he moved in. He'd kept her away before because this place revealed too much of what had happened to him without her.

She looked up to find him watching her closely, asking if she understood the things that were beyond words. She smiled and squeezed his hand. As he began going through his shelves she passed on into his bedroom.

Here there was more bleakness. A plain bed, a wardrobe, a bureau. No ornaments, photos, mementoes. Nothing to remind him of anyone he'd ever known. Not even herself, she realised with a pang of disappointment.

Suddenly she couldn't stand it a moment longer. She began pulling open drawers, seeking something, anything, to reveal his inner life.

And she found it.

It was all there together in the bottom drawer, starting with their wedding pictures. They were excellent, a gift from a photographer friend. There was the absurdly young-looking eighteen-year-old girl and the scrawny young man. She frowned at the sight of Jake. Where was the confident young god of her memory?

Had he really been this slightly loutish-looking individual with the unfinished air? And his expression, full of adoration for the girl beside him? Why hadn't she noticed that at the time? Perhaps because her own adoration had filled her horizons.

Over the years he'd taken his own pictures of her, and there was one where everything had come together perfectly. Focus, colour, pose were all brilliant, and in the centre was a girl, laughing with joy because the man she loved was giving her all his attention. Her head was thrown back and happiness seemed to pour from her. Jake had blown this one up and framed it to keep. And then he'd hidden it away in secret.

Now, she thought, she knew everything. But she was wrong. The drawer had two final secrets to yield. First was a pair of baby bootees, one larger than the other. Kelly stared at them a long time, wondering about this man whose heart was so much deeper than she'd suspected.

But it was the last item of all that made her cry: a blue furry elephant, his trunk knocked permanently out of shape on the day she'd thumped Jake with him.

Now she remembered him, that night in the park, saying, 'It was definitely Dolph the elephant. I know because I—because his trunk was always wonky after that.'

He knew because he'd kept him all these years, grieving for the child they'd lost as deeply as herself, but unable to say so. And perhaps grieving also for those early happy days that had gone. She bent her head and her tears fell on Dolph's fur.

She felt Jake's presence as he sat on the bed beside her, and his arms went around her.

'Don't cry,' he said. 'You can give him to your baby. He won't mind about the trunk.'

'It's not that,' she wept. 'It's everything—we had so much and we lost it.'

He drew her close and she sobbed freely on his shoulder. Now it was his turn to comfort her, and he did his unpractised best.

'I don't know what you want me to say,' he told her. 'I never really did. Perhaps we never could have kept what we had. We were both so young, and I was clumsy. You had all those exam passes and all I had was "front" and "attitude". I made them do a good job for me, but in the end they're not enough. When you got pregnant I was so relieved. It gave me the chance to tie you to me so that you couldn't escape. Not very nice behaviour, but I wasn't a very nice character. Look at me—' He'd taken up the wedding picture. 'I was a bit of an oaf in those days. You were the best thing that ever happened to me, so I grabbed with both hands.'

'I was—the best thing—you loved me?'

'I've never loved anyone in my life as much as I've loved you. And I never will. All I wanted was for you to love me, and somehow I could never quite believe that you did.'

'Love you?' she echoed, astonished. 'But Jake, I adored you. You must have known that. I positively hero-worshipped you.'

'Oh, yes,' he said quietly. 'I knew you hero-worshipped me, but that's not quite the same as love. It was quite scary. I kept waiting for you to discover that I had feet of clay. I reckoned you'd dump me when that happened. In the end you did, but I can't complain.

We had eight years, and that was more than I hoped for.'

At first she was too shocked to speak.

'But—but it wasn't like that,' she stammered at last. 'It was always me scurrying around in your shadow, afraid I was boring you. You achieved so much—'

'Only because you told me I could. I was a bum. I had a big mouth and I could talk my way into jobs, but I usually talked my way out again because I annoyed people by being too clever by half. Then I met you, and you actually admired me, which nobody had ever done before. If my name was mentioned people used to say, "Oh, him!"'

'Jake, that's not true—'

'It is true, but you never knew. You made me see myself through your eyes, believe that I could be what you thought me. And then when—when we broke up, you made me see myself through your eyes again, someone who'd taken everything and given back nothing. That's really why I agreed to the divorce. I reckoned you deserved to be free of me.' He gave a snort of self-condemning laughter. 'Even so, I convinced myself that you'd back off at the last minute. I never thought of your flying straight into the arms of another man.'

'I didn't, Jake, honestly I didn't.'

'What about Carl?'

'What about him? He's not my baby's father.'

He grew still, searching her face. 'Is that true?'

'It's true. Jake, you *know* who this child's father is. You do. You've always known, really.'

He shook his head helplessly. 'I don't know anything any more. It's no use asking me to work things out.

It's all gone. Everything I used to have or be, it's all gone.'

'No, it hasn't. You've still got me, you've still got our baby, and you've still got your talents.'

He barely seemed to hear her. He laid his hand over her swelling stomach, only just touching it.

'Our baby,' he whispered. 'Ours?'

'Yours,' she said softly.

She wished she could see his face, but his head was bent. Gradually he slipped to the floor, resting his head against the swell, and beneath her hands she could feel the violent shaking of his shoulders. She tried to speak, but the effort died. No words would be adequate. No words were needed. She put her arms as far around him as she could and held him quietly while he sobbed.

This might have been despair at an added burden, but her instincts told her that he was weeping for joy. Once she would have found that hard to believe, but they'd travelled far together in the last few months. He was clinging on desperately to anything that would keep him sane in the middle of chaos, and now he had new hope.

'Tell me again,' he said huskily. 'Say this is my child.'

'Darling, of course it's yours. Who else's could it be?'

'But I thought—'

'There was never anyone but you. How could there be? I divorced you because I thought I'd lost you already. When you turned up at the party I wanted you to see me as the belle of the ball, for the sake of my pride. But the truth was I still loved you, even though I wouldn't admit it to either of us. Afterwards, how could I tell you what that night meant to me?'

'Can you tell me now?' he whispered.

'I love you, Jake. I always have and I always will. This baby is yours, and I want you to be there, always, to be his father.'

'I'm not much of a bargain in my present state.'

'Stop talking about yourself like that,' she said fiercely. 'You're mine, and I'm never letting you go again. Clear everything out of this place. You're not coming back here. I'm taking you home for good.'

His answer was to lean his head against her breast, spreading his arms to encompass her and their child.

'I am home,' he said.

CHAPTER TWELVE

FOR a while practical matters held their attention. Jake put his flat on the market, finding a buyer at once.

'But I'd like to keep that money aside for a deposit on a proper home,' he said. 'This'll be a bit small when there's three of us.'

She agreed, but didn't say more, leaving Jake wondering how their future life was to be organised. For the moment it was enough that they were back together. When he looked into the future he saw several paths, all with turnings that he couldn't follow. Yet, strangely, the uncertainty didn't trouble him. Everything was in Kelly's hands, and there were no hands that he trusted more.

One day Kelly said, 'You're feeling a lot better, aren't you?'

'Yes, how did you know?'

'You've stopped talking like a robot. When you were at your worst the words came out sounding harsh and mechanical. Those pills the doctor gave you were good.'

'It wasn't the pills, it was you.' But it was true that the clouds were shifting. Now he found he could organise his work into some kind of order, and at last he had a synopsis of his book.

'We'll give it to a literary agency,' Kelly declared. 'Carl says his own is excellent, unless you'd rather—not Carl?'

'It's all right. I'm feeling kindly towards Carl these days.'

The result was an advance large enough to ease Jake's gloom some more, and enable him to work with an easy mind. Even so he knew that there was a question mark over his television future. His major commissions had come from Olympia, and that source must have dried up. She'd overlooked the first time he'd let her down, that night in Paris, but he supposed she'd wanted to add his scalp to her belt, and wouldn't easily admit defeat.

But what had happened in her apartment was another matter. He'd rejected her and exposed her to humiliation. He hadn't meant to. Every one of his actions had been driven by illness, but Olympia wasn't the woman to understand that.

Yet even this didn't trouble him. His career seemed to live on the fringe of his consciousness, taking any crumbs of attention he could spare it. The centre was here, where Kelly was growing larger every day.

'Are you keeping up to schedule on that book?' Kelly asked once. 'I know they wanted it fast.'

'I'm doing my best.'

'If you need some secretarial help I could—'

'No!' His yell was so loud that she almost dropped her cup. 'Don't even think of that. You've got your own work to do. Give it all your attention.'

'But I only—'

'I said no!'

'All right, all right,' she said hurriedly.

There was a silence. His mind had gone dark again, brooding over how close history had come to repeating itself. Once before he'd snatched away her chance of making her own success. Now she'd calmly offered him the opportunity to do it again. Sweat stood out on his brow.

'Hey, it's all right,' she said, giving him a little shake. 'Don't take everything so seriously.'

He took her hand. 'I'll try.'

'But get finished soon, because Olympia will be calling you.'

'Not her! She's not a forgiving lady.'

'No, but she's an ambitious one. Without you her ratings have fallen.'

He stared. 'How do you know that?'

'One of the lecturers on the media studies course does freelance work for her company, and he hears things. They've tried to find someone to be as popular as you, but they've failed. People have been asking her when they can expect you back. You can virtually write your own ticket.'

Kelly's tone gave no clue to her feelings. She was heavy now, calm and content with her child and her man. Nothing outside seemed to touch her very much.

He only half believed her about Olympia, but a week later the phone rang, and it was her. She was gracious, as always. The evening in her apartment might never have been.

'And you're well enough to start work again?' she enquired.

'Perfectly well.'

'I have a job that might interest you. It would mean—'

It was peach of a job, a major assignment that would put him right back at the top. Jake Lindley, the voice of truth, the man who brought you the facts: he could have it all back. Kelly had been right.

'Sounds interesting,' he mused in a non-committal voice that should have warned Olympia.

'Fine. I'll need you to leave next week—'

'Wait, I haven't said I'll do it yet. There's some unfinished business between us.'

'It surprises me that you want to mention it.'

'It doesn't surprise me that *you* want to avoid it, but I thought you might have some explanation for the Forest Glades stunt. It makes me sick that you actually tried to have me locked up to stop me going back to Kelly, but it's just possible that you thought you were acting for my benefit—'

'Just possible?' she yelped. 'You were out of your mind that night, on the verge of insanity. You needed help and I got it for you.'

'Well, you got me the wrong kind of help.'

'And what about me?' Olympia screeched. 'Talking about your wife and baby in front of those men! Do you know how you made me look?'

'If you hadn't sent for them it wouldn't have happened. It was pure spite.'

'Look, if I got it wrong that night I'm sorry—' Olympia spoke nervously. Without Jake the ratings had slumped badly.

'Skip it. Too late. And even if it hadn't been, there's no way I'd go away next week, or for several weeks. The baby's due soon and I've got to be here.'

'And people are supposed to just hang about indefinitely, waiting for you to be man enough to start work again?' demanded Olympia, letting her temper get the better of her caution.

'Man enough?' He savoured the words slowly.

'I didn't mean it like that—' She back-pedalled frantically.

'I don't really care how you meant it,' he said. 'You've made me realise that I've changed some of my ideas about what it means to be a man. I couldn't do this job, Olympia. Not next week, or the week after, or ever. I'm not watching my child's birth with a packed suitcase in one hand and a watch in the other. I'm not going to ask Kelly to hurry up because I've got a plane to catch. Nor am I going to be away after the birth, when she'll need me more than ever.

'I'm finished with dashing off around the world. I had my fun and it was great, but I had it at Kelly's expense, and now that part of my life is over.'

'You know what they'll all say, don't you?' Olympia asked nastily. 'That you've lost your nerve.'

'Let 'em.'

'Your career will never recover.'

'I'll make another career. I think I'm still sufficiently in demand for that. At any rate, it's time I found out.'

Olympia's voice was full of doom. 'Are you mad? You'll end up doing *gardening programmes*.'

'I like gardening,' said Jake, who'd never planted a seed in his life. 'I was thinking of getting a house with a garden. Goodbye, Olympia. And I mean *goodbye*.'

He hung up and sat brooding for a moment. When he looked up he saw Kelly standing in the doorway, smiling.

'You heard.' It was a statement, not a question.

'Yes, I heard. You turned down a job to be here when the baby's born.'

'To be *with you* when the baby's born,' he corrected insistently, helping her to the sofa. 'That's the most important thing in the world to me now—that the three of us should be together, not just then but later. Marry me, Kelly.'

'What did you say?'

Jake dropped to his knees beside the sofa so that his eyes, full of intensity, were on a level with hers.

'I want more than just living together; I want to marry you,' he said, so fervently that it came out sounding almost fierce. 'I always wanted to be married to you, right from the first. You were my love and my star, but you were also—' He hesitated.

'Also what?' Kelly asked, hardly daring to believe what she was hearing.

'The rock I clung to,' he said at last. 'It took me a long time to see it, but you were always my centre. You kept me safe. You always have. I began to understand when you started divorce proceedings. I was so arrogant I couldn't believe you'd really go through with it. I thought you'd see in time that you needed me. I wouldn't admit the truth to myself—that it was I who needed you.

'I dashed home, thinking I was in time to stop the divorce. I was going to say, "OK, you took it to the wire. Just tell me your terms for staying married." I'd have agreed to anything to make you call it off. But there was a mix-up about the date and by the time I got there we were already divorced.

'When I came to your party that night I was in a state of shock. And there you were, someone I didn't recognise. I began to see that I'd been wrong about everything. Suddenly I was at sea—no rudder, no compass, no Kelly.

'I didn't just lose my love, I lost my best friend, the person who primed me for every challenge. Suddenly I was faced with the hardest struggle of my life, and instead of advising me she was on the other side.'

'I wish you'd told me this,' she said softly.

'I might have tried if I could have talked to Kelly that night. But she wasn't there. She'd sent Carlotta in her place. And Carlotta—oh, boy!'

'You seemed to like her,' Kelly remembered tenderly.

'She gave me the best night of my entire life. Talk about sex personified. I hope—' He hesitated before saying almost shyly, 'I hope she and I will meet again. I'd be really interested in furthering our acquaintance. But that night she scared me. I suddenly saw what I was up against, how eager you were for your new life, how little reason you had to regret the old one. I saw the men who wanted you, all of whom would probably have appreciated you better than I had.

'And after that incredible night—the next morning I was waiting for you to say that everything was all right between us now, but all you said was that it was a perfect way to end our marriage. After that I couldn't get out fast enough, in case you guessed how close I'd been to begging you to take me back.'

'If only I'd known about this then,' she mused. 'And yet—'

'And yet it wasn't the right time.' He picked up her thought quickly. 'Not for either of us. We had a journey to make, to find each other again. I love you, and I want to marry you, and stay married to you for ever.'

She touched his face. 'That's what I want too.'

'Then let's do it now, at once.'

'Darling, we can't—'

'We can if we get a special licence.'

'But the baby's due any day.'

'That's why I want to hurry. I want us to be married before the baby comes. It's not something I can explain—it's just an irrational feeling. Marry me, Kelly, please.'

'All right,' she said, loving him for his urgency. 'Just as soon as it can be fixed up.'

'I'll do it now,' he said, jumping up. 'Let's see if my old contacts are still good.'

His luck held. One contact knew how a special licence could be obtained fast, and got working on it.

'But can we get a booking in the register office at the last minute?' Kelly asked anxiously.

'We're not going to a register office. We're marrying in church.' He seized her hands. 'I'm going to make up for last time. I can't give you the white dress and bridesmaids, but I can give you the church and the clergyman.'

He started dialling furiously.

'Don't tell me one of your contacts knows a clergyman?' Kelly asked.

'Nope. One of my contacts *is* a clergyman, and he owes me a favour.'

In a shorter time than she would have believed possible she found herself set to be married in two days' time. She was dazed, feeling the world spinning out of control about her. But one glorious fact stayed constant at its core. Jake loved her more than ever, and was racking his brains for ways to please her.

The clergyman turned out to be the Reverend Francis Dayton, who agreed to marry them as soon as the licence arrived. He was in his nineties, and long retired, but he assured them there would be no trouble about 'borrowing' a church.

'I'll just lean on one of my boys,' he said conspiratorially.

His 'boys' turned out to be his two middle-aged

sons, both of whom had followed their father into the church and had parishes locally.

Kelly had immediately warmed to the Reverend Dayton. Despite his age he had sparkling eyes, and seemed to regard it all as an adventure.

With the arrival of the licence everyone swung into action. Carl was giving the bride away and Marianne, his sister, got to work on Kelly's appearance.

'But what are you going to do about my bulk?' Kelly said, indicating her enormous size.

'This,' Marianne said, producing a voluminous blue velvet opera cloak. It had slits for the arms, and when it was fastened at the front the effect was surprisingly elegant.

Kelly's hair was a little longer now, and Marianne curled and teased it into a curving halo. Her eyes were delicately made up, but no make-up could improve on their true beauty, which was a glow of joy.

There was no veil, but Marianne fixed flowers in her hair, and there were matching flowers in the bouquets they both carried, for Marianne was also the brides-maid.

There was a pleasant cosiness about the wedding, which was to take place in a small chapel just off the main church, where five people would be just the right number. The elderly clergyman would double as best man, while Carl and Marianne would also be witnesses.

As she began the short journey down the aisle, on Carl's arm, Kelly had a clear view of Jake standing near the altar, his eyes fixed on her. At first she felt like a baby elephant, but as she neared Jake and saw the look on his face she forgot herself. This was the man she loved, and who loved her. They had almost lost each other but they'd come together again, because that was how they were meant to be.

There was a smile on his lips, but it was nothing to the smile in his eyes. On the night of their passion she'd seen his face glowing with an intense emotion, but it had been admiration for her slinky figure and sexual allure. Now she was heavy with their child and admiration had been replaced by adoration.

He reached out his hand to take hers and draw her forward. The Reverend Dayton coughed and began to read the service.

'Dearly beloved…'

In no time at all, it seemed, Jake took Kelly's hand in his while the priest asked him if he would have her for his wedded wife, forsaking all others as long as they both lived. His face was pale but determined as he said, 'I will.'

Then the same question to Kelly, but instead of her answer there was only silence. They all stared at her, first in bewilderment, then aghast as they saw her face taut with pain.

'I'm sorry,' she said breathlessly. 'Not—good—timing.'

'You don't mean—?' Jake asked.

''Fraid so. And that's the second one. They're coming fast. Jake—'

'My car's outside,' Carl said. 'Quicker than an ambulance.'

Kelly gasped again and held onto Jake. 'Our wedding—'

'You leave that to me,' the Reverend said. 'Which hospital?'

Bewildered, they told him, and he raced off, gathering his skirts up and calling out, 'Beat you to it.'

Jake and Marianne helped Kelly out of the church while Carl raced ahead to the car. By the time they reached him he had the engine running. Marianne joined him in the front while Jake sat in the rear, his arms about Kelly, his face full of apprehension.

'I shouldn't have insisted on this,' he muttered. 'It was too much for you.'

'No, no, it was a lovely idea,' she protested. 'I wanted it too.' She drew in her breath sharply as the next pain came.

'Was that another one?' Carl called over his shoulder.

'Yes,' Jake said tensely. 'You're the one who knows all about this. What does it mean?'

'It means we'd better hurry.'

He slammed his foot down and the car speeded up. Even so they were easily overtaken by a motorcyclist, his head obscured by a dashing helmet, his vestments flapping in the wind.

'Was that who I think it was?' Marianne asked, thunderstruck.

'Of course it was,' Kelly said, breathing hard. 'Oh, darling—' her arm tightened around Jake's neck '—we always said we were crazy, and it's catching. Everyone around us gets crazy too.'

'Kelly, I don't believe you're actually finding this funny!' Jake growled.

'But of course it's funny—and happy, and glorious and wonderful—the most wonderful thing that ever happened.'

At the hospital everything was ready for them, the Reverend Dayton having arrived first and alerted the maternity unit. Now a nurse was preparing to take a firm line with him.

'I'm afraid you really can't—' she started to say.

'Yes, he can.' Kelly clutched the old man's hand. 'I want him.'

'So do I.' Jake backed her up.

Another pain tore Kelly, but she waved away gas and air. She had something important to do first.

'Quickly,' she gasped.

While the nurses prepared her the elderly clergyman went into action. 'Wilt thou have this man to thy wedded husband…?'

'I will,' she said firmly.

Then it was Jake's turn. 'I, Jake, take thee, Kelly, to my wedded wife…'

Her senses were swimming, and all she heard clearly was, 'To love and to cherish till death do us part.'

That was how it would be now. Until death. They had tried leaving each other, and it didn't work. For ever was the only option left.

Through mounting waves of pain and joy she claimed him as her husband and held out her hand to receive the ring. The Reverend guided them quickly through the final rites before pronouncing, 'Forasmuch as Jake and Kelly have consented together in holy wedlock…I pronounce that they be man and wife…'

Man and wife. Kelly smiled her thanks at the old man as he waved and whisked himself out of the room, taking Carl and Marianne with him.

It was exactly nine months since the day of their divorce, and their son was urgently demanding to be born.

'I'm so glad we did that first,' she murmured. 'Afterwards wouldn't have been the same, somehow.'

Jake nodded and dropped a kiss on her forehead. An ache in his throat was making it impossible to speak.

His whole world had turned upside down. The things that had seemed important before had become trivial. Only this mattered—this moment, this woman, this child that they had created together.

It was the birth Kelly had longed for, with Jake beside her, sharing the experience. Unlike most first babies this one came quickly, and in a few minutes her son was in her arms.

'He's like you already,' she whispered. 'Impatient, rushing to get to the action fast.'

'That's something I'll have to warn him about. It's too easy to miss the things that matter.'

'He won't take any notice of warnings, not your son.'

'My son,' he said in wonder. 'Our son. Is it really possible?'

'Anything's possible, my love. Or we would never have found each other again.'

The Reverend Francis turned up, beaming, next day, to complete the paperwork and entertain her with the story of how he'd swept up to the hospital, yelling, 'Where's the maternity unit.'

'They took one look and nearly arrested me,' he said with deep satisfaction. 'I got stopped by the police too. They thought I was a Hell's Angel. I haven't had so much fun in years. And you're really going to call this little fellow Francis? Well, well! I'll be off now. Here's your husband.'

Jake had one more surprise for her. He'd arrived with his arms full of books.

'What are all these?' she asked when he'd kissed her.

'You have all that coursework to finish before the

term starts,' he said, 'and you should be working on them right now.'

'Right now? Have you forgotten how I spent yesterday?'

He sat on the bed, taking her hands in his. 'I'll never forget yesterday as long as I live. And it would be easy, wouldn't it, to say that now we've got the baby we don't need more?'

'Yes,' she said blissfully. 'Who needs anything else when they've got a baby?'

'But darling, I don't think it will last—not for you. You still want college, and studying. You might not think so at this moment, but that need will come back, and if you lose ground now you won't ever recover it. Those marks for your coursework count towards your final degree—if you don't do well you'll regret it the rest of your life. Believe me, you will.'

'You seem to understand me very well,' she said tenderly. 'Jake, it's sweet of you to think of this, but what else can I do?'

'Get someone else to look after little Francis while you study.'

'Oh, no, I don't want a stranger caring for my baby. And I don't think we can afford it.'

'The person I have in mind isn't a stranger, and he comes very cheap. Free, in fact.'

They looked at each other.

'But do you know anything about babies?'

'I wonder you dare to ask after those parenting classes you put me through. I've read the same books as you. I know as much theory as you, and I have the same amount of practical experience. In other words—none.'

'You crazy man,' she said in wonder. 'I think you actually mean it.'

'Of course I mean it. "Jake Lindley, Super Hero", is a man of many parts. Yesterday he saved the universe. Today he changes nappies—the ultimate challenge.'

'Are you saying you're going to change nappies?'

'Are you saying you think I couldn't manage it? It'll be hard, but I'll rise to the occasion. I'll suffer, I'll probably gag, but I shall overcome.'

She gave a watery chuckle. 'But darling, there's more than just looking after the baby.'

'I know. I'll look after you and Francis *and* I'll do the housework as well.'

He meant it. It was incredible, but he meant every word. Now she realised that she was only just beginning to understand the heart of the man. He'd been through the fire, emerging stronger and wiser. But one thing hadn't changed. He was all hers. He always had been, if she could have seen it. But she'd been through the fire with him, and her eyes were opened.

'It's all right, isn't it?' he asked, troubled at not being able to read her face.

'Everything's wonderful. It's just that I can't see you as a house-husband.'

'You don't think I'll look good in a frilly pinny?' He smiled. "Neither do I. This is just a short-term solution. We'll find a house and get some permanent help so that you can concentrate on your college course. But even then I'll still do some of the chores. This is my baby too, and I don't want to be left out. When we've got the routine going I'll start work on my next book.'

'But that could take ages, and you ought to be thinking up ideas for that now.'

'Kelly, darling, look at what's under your nose. I've just *had* the idea for the next book. Jake Lindley— House-husband. It'll be a best-seller.' His smile faded. 'That's the secondary consideration. The important thing is to be there for you. I failed you once. I swear I'll never do it again.'

He leaned down to the cradle and scooped his son up into his arms. The baby was so tiny, but Jake seemed to adjust instinctively, and when he'd settled the child he looked into his face, receiving back a stare as direct and challenging as his own.

'I thought one of those books said newborn babies couldn't focus their eyes just at first,' he said.

'I don't think they can.'

'Our son can. Look at him. He can see me and he knows who I am.'

'Jake—'

'No, look. He's bright, this one. Don't take any notice of her, my boy. Women don't understand, but we understand each other, don't we?'

'Oh, really?' she queried, watching them in a passion of tenderness.

'We'll do this book together, son. You'll provide me with the raw material and I'll write it up. If I run short of inspiration you can just poo or do something else interesting. We'll be a great team, and I'll give you Dolph as your share of the profits.'

'You meanie!' Kelly protested. 'He'll be doing all the hard work.'

Jake grinned at her, with more real amusement in his face than she'd seen for weeks. At last the clouds were lifting from both their lives. Now they could see the way ahead, and it was flooded with light.

A brand-new miniseries from

HARLEQUIN®
Romance®

Welcome to

High Society
Brides

Rich or royal…it's the wedding of the year…
and you are invited!

Live the drama and emotion of the most thrilling,
exclusive weddings that are about to take place, in:

January:
THE SHEIKH'S PROPOSAL
Barbara McMahon (#3734)

March:
BRIDE FIT FOR A PRINCE
Rebecca Winters (#3739)

Look out for star authors
Jessica Steele, Liz Fielding
and Sophie Weston
who will also be featured in
HIGH SOCIETY BRIDES
throughout 2003!

For better, for worse...
these marriages were meant to last!

They've already said "I do," but what happens
when their promise to love, honor and cherish
is put to the test?

Emotions run high as husbands and wives discover
how precious—and fragile—their wedding vows
are...but their love will keep them together—forever!

Look out for the following in

MAYBE MARRIED by Leigh Michaels
(#3731) on-sale January

THE PRODIGAL WIFE by Susan Fox
(#3740) on-sale March

And watch out for other bestselling authors appearing
in this popular miniseries throughout 2003.

Available wherever Harlequin books are sold.

If you enjoyed what you just read,
then we've got an offer you can't resist!

Take 2 bestselling
love stories FREE!

Plus get a FREE surprise gift!

Clip this page and mail it to Harlequin Reader Service®

IN U.S.A.	**IN CANADA**
3010 Walden Ave.	P.O. Box 609
P.O. Box 1867	Fort Erie, Ontario
Buffalo, N.Y. 14240-1867	L2A 5X3

YES! Please send me 2 free Harlequin Romance® novels and my free surprise gift. After receiving them, if I don't wish to receive anymore, I can return the shipping statement marked cancel. If I don't cancel, I will receive 6 brand-new novels every month, before they're available in stores! In the U.S.A., bill me at the bargain price of $3.34 plus 25¢ shipping & handling per book and applicable sales tax, if any*. In Canada, bill me at the bargain price of $3.80 plus 25¢ shipping & handling per book and applicable taxes**. That's the complete price and a savings of 10% off the cover prices—what a great deal! I understand that accepting the 2 free books and gift places me under no obligation ever to buy any books. I can always return a shipment and cancel at any time. Even if I never buy another book from Harlequin, the 2 free books and gift are mine to keep forever.

186 HDN DNTX
386 HDN DNTY

Name	(PLEASE PRINT)	
Address	Apt.#	
City	State/Prov.	Zip/Postal Code

* Terms and prices subject to change without notice. Sales tax applicable in N.Y.
** Canadian residents will be charged applicable provincial taxes and GST.
  All orders subject to approval. Offer limited to one per household and not valid to current Harlequin Romance® subscribers.
  ® are registered trademarks of Harlequin Enterprises Limited.

HROM02   ©2001 Harlequin Enterprises Limited